THE LOST TEMPLE OF KARTTIKEYA

MLR Press Authors

THE LOST TEMPLE OF KARTTIKEYA

LAURA BAUMBACH

mlrpress

Published by
MLR Press, LLC
3052 Gaines Waterport Rd.
Albion, NY 14411

Visit ManLoveRomance Press, LLC on the Internet:
www.mlrpress.com

Cover Art by Deana C. Jamroz

Printed in the United States of America.
ISBN# 978-1-934531-93-8

First Edition
2008

CHAPTER ONE

Brandon King wasn't sure what woke him, but sleep had suddenly slipped away as quickly as the sweaty T-shirt and worn jeans he had tossed in the corner of the room hours ago. Now, he lay naked on his belly, senses hyperalert, his service revolver in his hand under his pillow. He almost had the gun drawn when the familiar scent of a certain aftershave tickled his nose. It was mixed with the smell of scotch, but it was still easy for him to recognize. He'd been enticed by the scent of it from the first day he met the man who wore it.

The jingle of a belt buckle and zipper sliding down made him rise up off the pillow and turn his head. Only a large, unsteady shadow could be seen by the open bedroom door, struggling out of clothing. A faint glow from the bathroom nightlight threw just enough light for Brandon to make out the buff lines of his lover, and senior partner, Phil Gates.

"Phil?"

A grunt and the thud of a shoe hitting the floor answered him.

"I thought you were ... busy tonight." Still on his stomach, he released his hold on the gun and slid it deeper under the pillow.

The movement stopped and the shadow straightened. "Well, fuck." The deep voice was harsh, rough like driftwood. It made Brandon's cock jerk. "You want me to fucking leave?"

"No, no." Unreasonable panic squeezed his chest, like it did every time Phil said something about leaving. Brandon was always sure if the older man left, it would be for good. "I didn't mean that. I just ... you said ... you and ..." He let it drop, reluctant to say Phil's fiancée's name out loud, let alone mention that Phil *still* had a fiancée three months into *their* relationship. "Forget it. I'm just ... still half asleep."

"I'll see if can't wake up your other half." The thud of the other shoe hit and then a heavy, hot body slid under the sheets from the foot of the bed to cover him. Sharp bites nipped his ass and moved along his spine as Phil's weight pressed him into the mattress.

"I love your little ass, Brandy. So tight, firm, and all *mine.*" Powerful hands kneaded his ass cheeks, almost bruising in their strength.

"Fuck you, Phil." Brandon grimaced into the pillow, but didn't shove the hands away, his hips rising up involuntarily into the rough caress.

"Not likely, darling." Phil bit Brandon's neck and then nuzzled his ear, teasing Brandon's supersensitive skin along his jawline.

It sent a ripple of pleasure through his body. Brandon couldn't help but moan. He blinked and shivered as the bedside light flicked on and Phil's thickly muscled body stretched over his to reach the table. Phil liked to look at Brandon's trim, nearly hairless body. It made Brandon self-conscious, but he was growing used to it.

"Fucker."

"I fully intend to be. And it's all for you, Brandy boy."

"Stop calling me that." It was a weak, token protest.

It was met with a soft, tolerant chuckle of dismissal.

"Can't. You're as intoxicating as it is, babe."

Despite the hated nickname being huffed in his ear along with the pungent fumes of expensive scotch, Brandon's cock had hardened at the other man's first touch. His pulse rocketed and he felt his skin flush with excitement. Even that electric buzz of approaching orgasm had already started deep in his belly.

Phil was ten years older and far more experienced than Brandon. Newly promoted to detective in the LAPD Burglary Division, Brandon was still learning the ropes. Domineering and persuasive, Phil had become Brandon's willing mentor at work.

A closeted bisexual, Phil was engaged to lawyer Susan Lista when he and Brandon became lovers, which was shortly after becoming work partners. Three months later, Phil's engagement ring was still on Susan's finger and his cock was still up Brandon's ass.

Brandon knew he should break it off, but coming from a string of unsatisfying short-term affairs, he was eager for the comfort of a relationship. Phil had charmed, seduced, and overwhelmed Brandon, both at work and in the bedroom. And he still did.

He overlooked Phil's controlling nature, preferring to think of his lover as merely a "take charge" kind of guy. After all, the man was a cop. Cops always had to have control, didn't they? He ignored the fact that he was one, too, and took a submissive role. He also ignored the fact that he was number two in a relationship in which he desperately wanted to be the one and only.

Problem was, when Phil was with him, he made Brandon feel like he was the only one in the man's life. Brandon sometimes had to struggle to remember the truth. Like now.

Brandon found he was constantly amazed at how much he was willing to forgive Phil. Brandon had pulled a few extra hours of duty, knowing Phil always spent Wednesday nights with Susan. His feelings bruised, like they always were any night Phil spent his free hours with Susan, he had worked late and long, leaving himself only a few hours between shifts. Now, Phil was here, wide-awake and amorous, only a few hours before they both needed to be up and at work.

An objection rolled up to Brandon's lips, but Phil began massaging his shoulders and neck with one hand while his talented mouth and tongue explored Brandon's ear and hairline.

"Ah, Christ. That feels great, Phil."

Phil moved the sensual assault down Brandon's spine, leaving a trail of heated kisses and long, rough laps of his tongue. Brandon shifted to allow his cock more room, the shaft rising to full engorgement by the time Phil had slid down to taste Brandon's ass.

A wet jab at his asshole made Brandon jerk and push back, encouraging more of the same. Phil ignored the silent request and lavished a series of licks and sucking kisses over the sensitive crease and the puckered skin around Brandon's entrance.

Spreading his legs wider, Brandon clenched the sheets and held on. He knew once Phil started eating him out, it would be a slow, agonizingly delightful event that would leave him on the verge of coming. Phil wouldn't stop until he had Brandon begging for more. And Brandon knew he would. Nobody rimmed like Phil did. No one made him feel the way this man did. It made all the negatives of the relationship worth overlooking most of the time. At least, at times like this.

His exhaustion fell away as his libido took over. Brandon swayed with the movement of the mattress as Phil got comfortable between his widespread legs. He grunted when thick arms slid under his thighs, drawing them up slightly. His cock was fondled and then angled down between his legs, then his groin was shoved down as Phil's callused hands fingered his ass cheeks and pulled the tight globes open.

Cock pointing south, trapped against the sheets, Brandon felt his tightening sac resting against the base of his hard shaft, cool air reaching flesh usually untouched. Phil's fingers walked their way closer to his wrinkled hole, exposing his entrance. Brandon could see in his mind how he must look, laid out, spread, his most private parts revealed and vulnerable. He shivered at the vision and the movement rubbed his cockhead against the sheets again, creating a spot of pre-cum wetness under it.

The first touch of Phil's wet, stiff tongue at the top of his ass crease made Brandon gasp into the pillow. His hand brushed the butt of his gun; he moved the cold steel farther out of reach. He grunted once then pressed his lips together to shut in the cry, which wanted to escape. It wasn't good to be this excited this quickly. Phil would only make him wait that much longer for a release if he thought he had him on the brink of orgasm this soon.

The tongue slithered up his spine a little and then disappeared between low, husky words that ghosted against his spine.

"That's it, lover. Talk to me. Let me hear you." Phil's tongue ran down the hot crease of Brandon's ass and circled the dark pucker of his hole, flicking at the edges, but not pushing past them. Once the opening was wet and slick, Phil lavished more wetness on the sensitive strip of flesh between asshole and scrotum before moving to Brandon's taut balls and trapped rod.

This time, at the touch of Phil's tongue, Brandon swore out loud and jutted his hips up and down, seeking more.

"Fuck!"

"Not yet. But soon, baby. I need a taste of your sweet ass first."

Brandon's balls were suddenly swallowed into what felt like a hot, wet cave, and then slowly allowed to ooze out between

Phil's lips. A puff of warm breath blew over the globes when they were released, making them crinkle and draw up tighter.

Cool wetness dripped down onto his pinned shaft. Brandon squirmed, moaning as it was licked away like icing and spread over his eager cock. Phil's fingertips kneaded his ass, lightly touching the entrance ring of nerves and muscle. Lips caressed the smooth flesh and teased the underside of his cockhead, teeth grazing over the flared rim and tapered tip. Brandon felt Phil's tongue explore the slit, lapping away the beads of pre-cum he knew pooled there.

"Christ, Phil." He groaned and shivered. "I need you."

"I know, baby, I know." There was a note of smugness to his tone, but the accompanying kisses and enticing caresses made it all acceptable for Brandon. "You'll have me. Soon."

Smooth warmth enveloped his shaft's head and any anger over Phil's egotistic tone fled in the face of sexual bliss. Phil's tongue, teeth, and lips lavished attention on Brandon's tip and shaft until he was squirming on the sheets. Hungry for more than that one small spot of stimulation, he reached back and spread his own ass, hoping to entice Phil's tongue upward. He clenched and unclenched his ass, feeling his puckered hole wink open and closed, a siren call to Phil's obsessive desire to lick ass.

Slowly, a hot trail of sharp nips and soothing licks worked their way up his shaft and over his balls, then settled on the sensitive strip of flesh that led to his entrance. Once there, they lingered and teased, darting up to his hole then back.

"Christ, Phil. Please! You're driving me nuts here."

"Mmmm. Nuts. Good idea." The hot breath and stiff, wet tongue moved back down to his balls. Brandon groaned in frustration and pleasure. They were sucked and kissed, jiggled and squeezed, then vacuumed into Phil's mouth for a final bath and suckle. Phil didn't release them until Brandon let go of his cheeks and knotted his hands in the sheets, his moans filling the bedroom.

Callused fingertips ran through the new sheen of sweat on his skin. "Anxious, Brandy? Want my tongue inside you? Up your ass? Hmmm?" Brandon felt the bed dip as Phil crawled closer. "I'm here for you, lover."

"Fuck! Come on, Phil." Brandon hated to beg, but he knew Phil liked it. It fueled the big man's lust to inferno levels. Brandon hated pleading, but he liked Phil raging and hot, so he begged. He pushed his ass higher, into Phil's face. "Fuck me. Please."

"Jesus, what a great ass." Brandon felt his ass cheeks kneaded, rough and bruising as Phil kissed the apple of each one. "But tongue first, lover. Cock second."

Brandon grunted and tensed as Phil's rough, broad tongue lapped over his hole. The rhythm was slow, torturous, and so good, he couldn't keep a moan from escaping. The lapping turned to wet, hard strokes as Phil's tongue went from flat and lazy to stiff and penetrating. The wrinkled edges of his opening spasmed and flared as Phil stroked and thrust his way over and past them. Sudden slurping sounds filled the air as Phil sucked at the opening, wiggling his tongue in deep to stroke the hidden channel's entrance.

Brandon buried his face in the pillow, letting his whimpers catch in his throat. He relaxed and slid his legs further apart, surrendering to the moment and Phil's will. If he couldn't get fucked, this was the next best thing. The laps and jabs were timed just right, pushing Brandon toward orgasm then retreating, prolonging the pleasure and heightening his need.

The rhythm of Phil's tongue sped up, then disappeared altogether. Brandon jerked his face out of the pillow and looked over his shoulder, trying to see.

"Phil?" The pressure on his ass and hips hadn't changed so he knew Phil was still down there.

"I want a better angle."

About to shift to one side so he could make eye contact, Brandon yelped and grabbed at the sheets as his hips were pulled up and back. He rose to his hands and knees more as a defense against being bodily hauled into the new position. He was never fond of being shoved for any reason, but Phil liked control in bed and he had a way of making it worth the degradation of being treated like a sack of potatoes. Or a rentboy. Usually.

One glance over his shoulder at Phil's face told him he had accomplished his prior goal. Phil was flushed and sweating, the dim light of the bedside table making his skin glisten. The glow caught the glazed, hungry look in the big man's eyes. Brandon had a fleeting thought that he looked like a wild beast ready to pounce on a meal.

Phil's cock stood thick and full, purple from the tip to a third of the way down its curved, circumcised length. The root was buried in a nest of thick dark hair, his balls pendulous in their dark, rosy sac. His intense stare was locked on Brandon's raised and exposed ass. His gaze flickered up to meet Brandon's, his eyes darkening.

"I love this ass." He smoothed both his palms over the twin globes, his touch reverent and adoring, like a caress to a baby's cheek. "Love the feel. Love the smell. Love the taste." He bent down and buried his face between Brandon's cheeks, swiping long licks over the sensitive skin, teasing the pucker as his fingers spread the flesh wide.

Brandon groaned and pushed back, trying to impale himself on the invading muscle. The visual of Phil's tongue lapping his darkest reaches played behind his closed eyelids. He grunted and trembled when a finger nudged its way in beside the questing tongue. The stretch and burn set his nerves on fire like the threads of a fuse bursting into flame. They raced up from his ass to ignite the rest of his body in a backdraft of consuming passion. It was always like this with Phil. Overwhelming and mind-blowing. The man just knew how to touch him.

Brandon dropped his head down between his supporting arms and looked at his shaft. His cock jerked more erect, blood pounding along the fat veins on the underside, the head flushed red and dotted with creamy beads. Underneath his own tightly drawn up sac he could see Phil's shaft jutting down proud and thick, nestled against his dark scrotum. It looked like a sword ready to do battle. Brandon desperately wanted to offer his ass as a sheath.

"Oh, God." The finger slid in deeper, working open the tight ring, letting Phil's tongue slip in that little bit further to make Brandon's head reel and his belly clench. His ass spasmed and clamped down on the digit. The inner lining of his body clutched at it, trying to pull it in deeper. The thick tip grazed the nub of his prostate. Brandon moaned and panted through the flash of electric jolts that sizzled through him, his ass thrusting back, eager to have more of the same.

CHAPTER TWO

His skin was flushed; a sheen of sweat broke out across it, with his breath coming in tight grunts and pants. The outside world around him disappeared to gray and all Brandon could think about was Phil's mouth, Phil's tongue, Phil's hands on him, in him, the man's scent and presence surrounding him. There was nothing like this in the world. Phil made Brandon feel like he was the sexiest lover on earth, the sole object of the other man's desire. Even if it wasn't true.

Brandon shook the sudden thought of Susan from his head and let the building rush of rising orgasm overwhelm him. The jab, stroke, curl, and rub of wet tongue and callused fingertip over sensitive, untouched membranes were indescribable. All Brandon could do was pant and bite his lip. Eager for more, he grabbed his cock with one hand, but it was knocked away and replaced by a larger, stronger one. Phil ignored Brandon's pre-cum-smeared shaft to tug on his sac, one thumb roughly caressing the thin strip of perineum between balls and asshole.

Brandon felt the rim of his ass stretched downward and Phil's tongue slithered deeper. One wiggled thrust set off an explosion of light and thunder. Brandon's orgasm rushed up from the base of his cock to barrel out his untouched dick, stopping only long enough to trigger his ejaculation before squeezing past his pounding heart and erupting in a show of color and sound inside his head.

He knew he cried out, knew he had groaned and swore, because he always groaned and swore when Phil ate him out, but he didn't know how he ended up on his side with his one leg bent forward and Phil's condom-covered cock already nudging into his ass. It was more sudden than usual and it made Brandon gasp and tremble, his hole not quite ready for more so soon. His ass muscles spasmed and clenched, the burn and stretch intense.

Phil leaned down and covered Brandon's lips in a raw, rough kiss that swallowed down his moan of discomfort, and a startled protest lodged in the back of his throat. By the time Phil released his lips, the burn has become a nearly pleasant fire and the short strokes of Phil's long dick bumped the ring of fluttering nerves and muscles, causing bursts of pleasure to spark in the pit of his abdomen.

Phil nudged deeper and huffed a sultry breath of hot air against Brandon's neck. "Take a just a little of it, baby. Only a little."

The head of his cock popped through the ring of muscle guarding Brandon's hole, the rim flaring and contracting at the familiar intrusion.

"That's right, feel me spread your little hole wide. So hot, so tight." A long, exhaled breath hit the back of Brandon's neck. The hot words danced along his skin, cooling the wet patches left behind by Phil's lapping tongue. Brandon groaned and his hips bucked. Strong hands held him still, refusing to let Brandon have any control.

"Can you feel how thick I am? How hard you make me?"

Feeling the round, broad head of Phil's fat cock as it lay just barely inside the rim of his ass, Brandon groaned and flexed his back, shoving his ass backward to force Phil past the burning ring.

"Nope, nope." Phil's hands stilled Brandon's pumping hips. "You only get a little of me at a time, Brandy boy. I want you to feel every inch of me sliding in." He jutted forward, sliding deeper, but not by much.

Brandon wanted more, needed more. He clenched his ass and tried to encourage Phil to lose a little of his steely control.

He was rewarded with a sharp stinging slap on his ass and a nip to his shoulder.

"Jesus, Phil!" He knew there'd be teeth marks by morning.

A rough hand slid under his head and clamped loosely over his mouth, cutting off any further comments. After a moment, two of Phil's fingers slipped into his mouth and Brandon automatically began to suck on them, his lips and tongue mimicking the thrusts at his ass.

"Fuck! What you do to me." A deep groan vibrated through Brandon's bones, Phil's face pressed against the top of his spine. "That's right, babe, squeeze me, pull me in. Don't talk, just ride that iron cock."

Brandon sucked harder, lavishing his tongue over the fingers in his mouth, grunting and flexing his ass's muscles, trying to set up a matching rhythm between both his holes, eager to be filled, wanting to swallow Phil's cock as completely as he was able to swallow the flesh sliding in and out of his wet, slurping mouth.

"Not full yet, lover. Got more for you." Wiry hair scratched against Brandon's parted cheeks. The burn at his opening intensified as the fat base of Phil's hard dick finally pushed solidly home.

"Oh, Christ almighty, you feel good." There was a snuffled nudge at the side of his throat and Brandon felt a tongue lick its way up his neck and behind his ear. It rubbed and teased at the underside of his ear, making Brandon pull away. The mouth followed, teeth capturing his earlobe and pulling him back for more.

Phil stopped to pant and groan. "Can you feel me?' He thrust in harder and withdrew slowly, waiting at the end of the stroke with just the head of his prick inside the grip of Brandon's opening. The muscles fluttered and clenched wildly around the stout pole. Brandon groaned around the fingers in his mouth.

"Can you feel my rod stretching your sweet little hole? Can you?"

Unable to answer any other way, Brandon pulled his abdominal muscles tight and snapped his hips, impaling himself back on Phil's long, thick cock.

"Ah, baby! That's it, buck and ride. God, your sweet ass is the best."

Wanting more, Brandon began to thrust and grind, but Phil pulled his ass against his own groin and held him tightly in place. He grabbed Brandon's cock and slowly stroked it, a tender-rough grip that soothed and excited.

"Slow down. Not so fast. Enjoy the ride, Brandy baby. Take every inch. Feel every inch of me. In you, deep inside of you, where I belong." Phil started a slow, shallow thrusting that rubbed his dick's head over Brandon's prostate on the inward jab and made his hole burn and spasm on the outward stroke. Divine pleasure and pain with each cock thrust and poke.

The fingers in his mouth began a slow pumping action and Brandon gobbled them down deeper, licking and sucking like he expected them to shoot a reward down his throat like the one he was hoping for up his ass. The room was filled with wet, slippery sounds and the slap of flesh on slick flesh.

Brandon's dick jerked and hardened even more, the head swollen and wet with pearls of thick pre-cum that Phil smeared over its length with his busy palm.

"Tight, hot ass. Christ, I love this ass. Love you, too, baby. Love what your ass does to me." Phil's thrusts became longer and rougher, deeper and less controlled. He grunted between words and a layer of sweat on his chest made his skin stick to Brandon's back.

Phil's breath smelled of alcohol and his fingers tasted faintly of the sharp woodsy tang of brandy, like the man had stirred the amber liquid with them at one point in the evening before coming to Brandon's bed. He smelled and tasted like a man, bitter and bold and hard. Brandon loved it. He never wanted to have anyone else in his life. Phil was it, flaws and all.

A deep grunt and Brandon rocked forward as Phil picked up the pace of his thrusts. They were hard and rapid, stretching Brandon wide and filling him so far he felt the jab of blunt flesh far into his abdomen. His own orgasm started to climb up from his toes. He clamped his mouth around Phil's fingers, unable to do anything more elaborate than suckle like a newborn, starving baby. His entire focus was on the cock reaming out his ass, throwing his thoughts and emotions into total chaos.

"Is it burning yet? Is your tight little pucker screaming my name yet, Brandy boy? Can you feel the burn all the way up to the tip of your dick?"

A rough stroke and tight squeeze made sure Brandon did feel it. The sultry voice in his ear and the whispered urgings made his blood pound in his head and his face blush. Phil's groans and sighs punctuated his breathy questions and the combination pushed Brandon's desire over the edge from a slow burn to a speeding rush.

"Feel it in the pit of your stomach yet?" Phil's thrusts got harder, deeper. "You can, can't you? You can feel me in the center of you." He pulled out slowly, then rammed home again. "Deep inside of you. I know it." Somehow he managed to go even deeper. "I can feel your heart pounding against my dick."

Phil bit down on the curve of Brandon's neck and shoulder. He pulled his fingers from Brandon's mouth and used his hand to force Brandon's head sideways. Brandon's mouth sought out contact again, empty and lost with the fingers gone.

Phil kissed him, a deep, voracious kiss that sucked the air from Brandon's lungs and pulled his orgasm up from the base of his spine to spill out over Phil's stroking palm. Brandon cried out, but it was a muffled grunt and whimper, locked behind their sealed lips.

Phil hammered his cock in a rapid-fire action, then arched and froze, his shaft buried to his balls, Brandon stretched and stuffed to his core. Even with the condom Phil wore, Brandon could feel the heat of the load emptying inside his body.

Riding off the crest of his climax, Brandon came back to awareness, body automatically responding to the tongue still stroking his, Phil's kiss less hungry, but just as persistent.

When he finally broke away, Brandon's lips felt chapped and his jaw ached. It matched the raw burn of his roughly palmed cock and the ache in his still full ass. He was drained. Sex with Phil always left him limp, both physically and emotionally.

"Fuck," Brandon moaned as Phil pulled out, his dick still half-hard and full enough that Brandon's ass protested, spasming at the swift, sudden burn. Brandon's own cock was still cradled in Phil's warm, motionless hand.

Tight, strong arms wound their way around Brandon's body and the heat radiating off Phil's chest and groin burned into his back and ass like a branding iron. He felt owned. It felt so good, Brandon got lost in the comfort of it.

"Is that a request for round two?"

"Only if you're on the receiving end this time."

"Not likely." A fleshy poke in the back made Brandon grunt when Phil chided, "I think I'm the only one up for a second round and that makes you the receiver, baby."

The arms around him tightened and pulled him back closer to Phil's body. Brandon recognized the signs that Phil was settling down to sleep despite the hard-on nudging his back.

He'd never say it out loud, but Brandon craved this. This was when Phil was at his most affectionate, unguarded and unafraid to show his feelings by holding him, wrapping around him, and caressing him without the expected reward of sex. This was what made Brandon fall in love with Phil. He lived for these little moments, which made him forgive Phil all of the missed dates and unannounced midnight visits.

Phil palmed Brandon's spent cock in a playful tug. Brandon hissed and knocked the hand away, too sensitive and suddenly too tired for anything more. "Forget it. Game over. You win."

"Damn straight." Phil snuggled closer and planted his nose in Brandon's hair. "Like always."

Hot puffs of air warmed his scalp. The sensation sent a shiver down Brandon's spine. He concentrated on the feeling of being engulfed by the man, letting a small snort of amusement escape his dry lips.

"There's nothing straight about us." He felt Phil's body stiffen and the heat on his scalp disappear.

Moving away from Brandon's side, Phil leaned up on an elbow and gazed down at him, the dim light of the lamp making dark gouges out of the furrows in his tanned forehead. "What's that supposed to mean?"

Wanting to diffuse the conversation before the alcohol in Phil's system ran off with his mouth and he said something Brandon would regret later, he muttered, "It means... we're two men having sex and sleeping together." He found the courage to meet Phil's dark gaze. "Touching each other."

A noncommittal grunt answered him.

He ran a hand up Phil's bulging bicep nearest him and then trailed his fingers across the man's hard nipples. "I'm looking forward to next week when we can at least hold hands in public. It'll be nice to be vacationing someplace where we can be ourselves. You're going to love it; the Keys are great this time of year. "

"Yeah, about that." Phil abruptly sat up on the edge of the bed. He glanced critically back over his shoulder.

Brandon became acutely aware of his naked, sprawled state. He blushed and quelled the urge to cover himself with the sheet.

Phil's gaze lingered over Brandon's hips and the curve of his ass before he snapped upright and stood. When he turned around, his pants were halfway on. The zipper made a cold, final sound in the sudden stillness of the room. "I can't make it."

It took a moment before it clicked with Brandon what Phil was talking about. When it hit him, he could barely work a single word past the stunned disbelief and hurt that hit him full in the chest, freezing the air in his lungs. "What?"

"The trip to Key West. I know everything is set, but I can't go." Phil pulled on his socks standing up and scuffed his feet into his loafers.

"Phil?" It hurt to force the word out of his tightening throat.

"Susan wants me to go on a cruise with her." He pulled his shirt on and Brandon watched as Phil casually buttoned it up and smoothed out the wrinkles with his hands, seemingly unaffected by the distress Brandon heard in his own voice. "Down to Brazil to join her father for a week. He's a powerful man in some circles. He only gets a little time off for personal things. It's just bad timing that it's the same week as my vacation."

Brandon sat up on the edge of the bed, pulling the sheet into his lap when Phil's gaze dropped to focus on his groin, ignoring Brandon's face and, apparently, also his words. "*Our* vacation. We've been planning this for two *months*."

Grabbing a pair of loose pajama bottoms on the corner post of his bed, Brandon yanked them on and stood, anger taking over, pushing the hurt into the background. He couldn't believe what he was hearing. This trip was going to be the turning point in their relationship. He was going to make sure Phil had such a great time with him, he'd be sure to break it off with Susan. The only thing he could think of to say sounded adolescent and desperate, but he said it anyway.

"You promised."

Phil heaved a regretful-sounding sigh, but Brandon read his expression as nothing more than annoyed. "Sorry."

Brandon planted himself in front of Phil, fists balled up at his sides, hands aching with the urge to touch Phil and convince him that he didn't need anyone else besides Brandon to make him happy. Phil had said a hundred times he didn't want kids. There wasn't anything Susan could do for him that Brandon couldn't, besides give him a rich father-in-law.

His wounded heart was screaming, "Don't leave me," while his mouth was saying, "Are you fucking serious?" His heart sank when Phil's face hardened, the wrinkles in the corners of his eyes becoming tighter and his lips compressing into a pale line.

"Yeah, I am, Brandon." He stepped close and stroked a hand down the side of Brandon's face, one thumb caressing the top of his cheekbone. "Try to understand, baby. I'm still engaged to Susan. She wants me to spend some quality time with her old man, so I am." His thumb dropped down to trace the curve of Brandon's mouth. Brandon resisted the urge to suck it into his mouth and taste it.

Phil's voice softened and he lightly kissed Brandon's lips. "I think she's beginning to suspect there's more between you and me than a partnership at work."

Brandon closed his eyes and let the feeling of Phil's talented lips on his own soak into his brain. "So let her." His eyes fluttered back open as he felt the heat of Phil's larger body withdraw. "There *is* more happening between us than work, Phil." Frustration poured off him and ate at his soul. He watched helplessly while Phil mechanically checked his pockets to make sure the contents were still intact. "Isn't there?"

Phil spared him a quick, almost sympathetic glance. He bent to retrieve his wallet from the floor. "Brandon, I've been engaged to her for two years. I can't just walk away without an explanation."

"You said you were breaking it off with her months ago." Brandon hated the desperate tone to his voice. All the dreams he had for a future together with Phil felt like they were dissolving into nothing more than broken promises. He hated the condescending look on Phil's face even more than he hated begging.

"You know I can't do that. Not without a good reason."

"I'm not reason enough?" Voice huskier than he meant it to be, defeat battered against his rib cage with each beat of his slowly sinking heart. Brandon turned away, not wanting Phil to see the depth of the hurt in his eyes. He knew the other man could read him like a book by now. He felt exposed and more than a little used.

His ass clenched in time with his fists. For the first time, the lingering burn from his hole's stretched muscles made him feel cheap instead of loved. Phil wrapped his arms around Brandon from behind, making him jump at the unexpected intimacy. He was pulled back until the length of his body was pressed along Phil's chest and groin, the cold buttons and soft fabric of the other man's clothes rough against his still bare skin. His own chest felt branded by the heat of the arms embracing him, the physical warmth soothing some of his emotional pain. He'd always liked being held. It was one of his personal weaknesses, and Phil was a demonstrative man. One of the few pluses about a relationship with him.

"You know what I mean." Hot breath and a wet kiss nuzzled the flesh of his neck up into his hair, and Brandon couldn't resist leaning back into the comfort it offered. "A reason the guys at work can deal with." Another trail of kisses worked up the other side of his neck. Brandon closed his eyes and let himself believe Phil was being sincere. "I don't plan on winding up dead one day because my backup didn't show up. You know how much support gay cops get."

"I'd be outed, too." Fear knotted in the back of his throat, making his voice soft and husky, but Brandon swallowed it down. It lay like a iron ball in his stomach despite the strong hands kneading over his quivering abdomen. "We could deal with it together."

"That's not going to happen." The words were hard but Phil ran his hands under the elastic waistband of Brandon's pajama bottoms, his fingers caressing and easing away the sharp edges in his tone. "Look, I've been on the force for twenty years, I've got friends. I'd be okay. But you--" His fingers teased Brandon's cock, reawakening it, his touch sending a shiver up Brandon's spine. "--baby, you've just started out on the squad."

Phil's embrace tightened. "And you're a little guy." It was almost threatening, the restrictive, blatant force of the hold, the dark rumble of deep voice in his ear, the way Brandon had to push back a little extra to take a full breath. "You're built, sure, you're strong, but let's face it, babe, you're on the smaller side of the yardstick for cops."

Brandon's hands had been lightly resting on Phil's exploring forearms, but now he wanted to grab hold of Phil and throw the constricting arms off. His grip tightened, but then Phil teethed one of his earlobes, sucking it in time to the caressing motions on his skin under his pants, and the urge to escape ebbed. He squirmed, pushed against the solid arms, and rolled his head back into the seductive enticements at his ear. Sometimes his lower head did all the thinking for him.

"That's one of the things that attracted me to you; you fit in my arms so well." The nibbling at his ear turned to a trail of kisses that burnt their way down his neck and under his lifted jaw. "I'm just trying to think of you."

Phil's voice was whispered and heated, and ghosted over his wet skin like a tropical breeze. Brandon's skin flushed and his tongue grew lazy. "I..."

"Come on, baby." Phil urged Brandon to turn around with a prodding force that was persuasive but firm. Once they were face to face, Phil kissed him between sentences while his hands kneaded the cool flesh of his bare back, eventually gripping the firm globes of his ass. "It's just a few days, Brandy. I'll get back by next week and we'll still have time to spend together."

A wet nuzzle at his Adam's apple sent a shiver down Brandon's spine and filled his dick out to full length. Phil licked over the small knob on Brandon's throat, but he ignored the more obvious one in his tented pajama pants. "Maybe we can drive up the coast and find a little getaway to stay a couple of days. Alone with a view and room service, for three, maybe four days, okay?"

"Okay. Yeah, I guess." Fighting down his rising desire to ask for a blowjob, Brandon nodded, then started as Phil stepped away. The sudden loss of body warmth and contact left him with a cold feeling that went beyond his skin temperature. His very bones felt the resulting chill as icy fingers of dread tickled along his lower back. He knew he was losing a lot more than a few days of vacation time.

"Alrighty then. Great. It's a done deal." Phil ruffled Brandon's hair. The familiar gesture of affection now seemed trite and dismissive.

Brandon had to grab the fabric of his pajamas to keep from knocking Phil's hand away, but the hand didn't linger long. Phil had already moved to the bedroom door by the time Brandon had gotten control of the urge.

"I'll call you when I get back. Don't worry about making any plans; I'll take care of everything." Phil smoothed one hand through his short-cropped hair and gave Brandon a wink. "I'll call."

With that, he was gone. The thud of the front door shutting firmly echoed through the tiny apartment. Brandon felt the weight of the door closing as if it had closed on his chest. Phil hadn't needed to say good-bye out loud; Brandon could feel it in the silent air and the chill on his skin. If he didn't do something fast, he was going to lose Phil to Susan.

CHAPTER THREE

He was borderline late for his shift, but Brandon couldn't make himself care too much about it. His thoughts were stuck on the way Phil's curt departure had left him with a hollow feeling. His emotions were still too close to the surface, his head saying to get out of the relationship before his heart got trampled even more, but his dick and his heart were telling him it was just a phase Phil was going through. That he'd be back after a week, eager to resume their relationship. It was two-to-one odds, so his dick and heart won. Phil would miss him and be back just like he said he would.

Head down, eyes trained on his cluttered workspace, Brandon sloshed his extra large to-go cup of coffee on the only clean spot he could find and tossed a new bag of sugar-packed, sour fruit-flavored candies into the top drawer of the desk. Between the caffeine punch and sugar kick, he could work twenty-hour shifts without batting an eyelid. An ingrained routine since college, without either one on a daily basis, the headache he got was massive. He'd learned to keep his supplies in good reserve. Phil had his cigarettes and alcohol; he'd stick with his coffee and candy.

Sitting down behind his desk, he stared at the empty spot across from him and felt a small wisp of longing for his lover, then his gaze lit on the silver-framed picture of Phil and Susan and the longing melted away to be replaced with a combination of regret and anger.

"What's the matter, King? Missing your partner already, or is that pissed-off look jealousy? You know it's just me and you while our 'other halves' are out, don't you?"

Startled, Brandon jerked his gaze away from the photo and turned to find Gregg Holt perched on the far corner of his desk. He hadn't even heard the man approaching.

"Jealous?" Panic set in, Brandon's heart racing at the idea Holt had read his expression correctly and knew about his affair with his partner. His voice was tight and raw, with an unexpected husky edge to it. Fear was a wonderful thing. He felt the blood drain from his face. Despite being a cop, he'd never been all that good at keeping a poker face.

"Come on, Brandon. Phil's engaged to a beautiful, smart woman with a rich father and great connections. Now he's left you behind in this festering den of iniquity while he's off to sunny South America on vacation."

Holt opened Brandon's drawer and stole a few candies from the near empty bag left over from yesterday. He popped them into his mouth and chewed around his sentence. "I'd be jealous if my partner was doing that this week. Instead, I'm basking in the knowledge Briggs is having the nightmare of all vacations surrounded by his eight kids in sunny Florida amusement parks."

He swallowed and tried to snag the coffee cup, but Brandon smacked his hand away. Holt good-naturedly accepted the rebuff. "Weren't you supposed to be gone this week, too?"

Ignoring Holt's question, Brandon ran a nervous hand through his dark curls. He couldn't hold back the snort that exploded from his tight throat. "Yeah. Maybe a bit. The guy's got it good."

He hoped Holt didn't pick up on the biting sarcasm.

Tall and broad-chested, always dressed in a meticulous, dark designer suit, Gregg Holt was a good eight inches taller than Brandon, but he never made Brandon feel intimidated or lacking the way other larger men often did. Holt always seemed to treat everyone with equal respect and fairness. A black man who'd had to work harder to earn his way up the detective ladder than some of his peers did, Holt seemed to have a soft spot for Brandon's inexperienced ways and newbie standing. In many ways, he was more supportive than Phil was on a professional level. And his teasing sense of humor was a nice break from the curt dismissals of a few of the other detectives who were taking a bit longer to warm up to Brandon than he had hoped.

"Hell, yeah." Absentmindedly, Holt began shuffling Brandon's reports into piles, organizing items to create dark blotches of desktop between neat hills of white paper. "I heard the good attorney Lista got him to set the date. I didn't think that would happen for some time yet."

"Date? What date?" Brandon drew a blank. He squinted up at Holt, trying to discern what the man was talking about without making the same mistake he had made earlier by assuming too much.

He flinched when Holt reached over and tapped his forehead twice.

"You need to drink that coffee instead of just glare at it."

Huffing, Brandon grabbed the paper cup and brought it to his lips, but froze when Holt continued speaking.

"Wedding date, junior. You know, ringing bells, churches, rice, and expensive gifts. Mistake that I think it is, I can't wait. With her father's money, it'll be one hell of a party." A wistful sigh escaped the black man and he stared off across the room, apparently imagining the coming nuptials.

Despite the block of ice that had formed in his stomach, Brandon latched onto the one shred of hope Holt had offered. "Mistake? Why a mistake? Don't you think they'll be happy?" He gave a small forced laugh and his words were pointed and searching. "Does Lista have a boyfriend hidden somewhere?"

"No, but…" Holt looked down at the pile of paper clips he was gathering, studied them a moment, then caught Brandon's gaze and held it, his expression nonjudgmental but slightly guarded, as if he wasn't sure how Brandon would react to what he was about to say. "…rumor has it your partner does."

Heart frozen in his throat, Brandon could only stare over the top of his coffee cup. His heart didn't start beating again until Holt dropped his gaze and quietly added, "At least he used to."

Holt sighed and glanced around the subdued bullpen. Brandon's gaze followed his. More detectives were arriving as the workday started, but they were isolated enough to safely continue the conversation without anyone else hearing.

He flinched slightly when Holt broken into his thoughts, voice lower and darker than before. "You're new. You're his partner. Phil's an okay guy, but he thinks with his dick a lot of the time. You should know this." His concerned gaze latched onto Brandon's face and Brandon felt a wave of sympathy from the man.

"There's been talk about him having male lovers on the lowdown for years." Holt's eyes narrowed and his lips pulled into a thin line. "Don't get me wrong; I don't care what any man does outside of working hours, as long as it's legal, but I don't think it's fair to the lady involved."

Holt suddenly straightened up and stood, smoothing imagined creases out of his suit coat, fingers automatically checking that the buttons were in place. Holt's gaze flickered over Brandon. "Or the guy on the side." He turned to watch a heavyset uniformed sergeant come toward them with a call sheet in his outstretched hand. He quietly added, "I'm just saying, you know?"

Stunned, Brandon gulped his coffee, choking a bit on the acid liquid that had gone cold already. He wasn't sure if Holt was hinting he suspected Brandon was gay, involved with Phil, or just concerned the man's green partner would be taken by surprise at Phil's closeted sexuality. Maybe he meant to say all of it. Brandon couldn't tell, but he sure as hell wasn't going to ask. He was saved from stuttering out a half-assed, noncommittal comment by the sergeant's lumbering arrival.

"Captain says you two are working together while your partners are on leave time." Holt nodded, while Brandon wiped a splash of coffee from his chin. "This call just came in. A burglary over in the Clifton Fields district. Half their division is out with the flu, so they asked for backup from us and the cap gave it to them. You two are next up on the roster." He shoved the report into Holt's hand and turned away, calling over his humped shoulder, "They expected you twenty minutes ago. I'd move if I were you. Those rich guys like to scream to the mayor when they lose so much as a cuff link, let alone a priceless artifact nobody's ever heard of."

"Artifacts." Holt raised his well-manicured eyebrows. "Intriguing." Giving Brandon a shrug and a teasing grin, he waved an arm in a sweeping gesture toward the exit. "After you, my King."

"Great. Role-playing and sarcasm this early in the morning." Brandon downed the remains of his cold coffee, tossed the cup in the wastebasket for a two-point score, and grabbed a handful of candies from the new bag of sweets -- his usual breakfast of champions.

If Phil were here, he'd chide him for his lax dietary habits, then the bastard would steal half of the candy throughout the day. Brandon grabbed a few extra just for spite. "I need to stop for more coffee on the way, okay? I'll need it if we have to interview the high society crowd."

"Don't worry, my King." Faking a cultured English accent, Holt tilted his nose in the air, a twinkle in his eye and a wry grin on his handsome face. "I'll interview the lords and ladies. You can handle the peasantry." He winked, bowing again, indicating Brandon should lead the way toward the exit. As Brandon passed him, Holt added, "You just take the notes down on your royal notepad, your highness."

A sense of humor was a nice change from Phil's usual dominating bluster, but Brandon gave Holt a glare as he passed in front of him anyway. "You're going to be an asshole all day, aren't you?"

"Yes, my King." Holt nodded and his grin widened. "Probably all week, too."

"You're buying the coffee."

"Ah, your first royal decree." Holt's voice held just the right note of praise and kingly worship.

"It's going to be a long fucking week." Despite himself, Brandon smiled, his mood lifting slightly. He pushed all thoughts of Phil's absence and accelerated marriage plans to the back of his mind, hoping to keep them there for the rest of the workday. A nice, clean, high-class burglary was just what he needed to get his thoughts off his faltering love life.

◊ ◊ ◊ ◊ ◊

"It grants your heart's fondest desires." Audra Phelan glanced at the empty display case, then transferred her penetrating gaze to Brandon's face. He could feel the intensity of it studying every angle and furrow in his expression. It was unnerving, as if she could see his aching heart straight through his skin. "At least," she softly added, "according to the legend."

"Legend? Fairy tales for broken hearts?" Brandon scoffed, but the unflinching certainty in the tall, prim woman's expression and body language made him stare at the small gold statue huddled in the midst of an entire glass wall of statues all the same.

There were at least a dozen artifacts in the case. One bronze cauldron, a crystal flacon, an elegant totem, a glass octopus, and a beautiful primitive carving made out of some raw yellow-orange material he didn't recognize. They all were fascinating to look at, beautiful, artistic, and varied, but the golden god was the one that drew his attention the most. It was almost like the statue had an unseen magnetic pull that tugged on the iron in his very blood.

Housed in the sitting room where they were conducting interviews about the robbery, the statue's golden hues and intricate design of six legs, six arms, and three heads on a jewel-encrusted body sitting astride a colorful peacock, had pulled Brandon to it and now he couldn't walk away.

"If so, it's a very powerful fairy tale."

That same vaguely knowing tone in the woman's voice reached out and squeezed Brandon's gut. It was like she had some secret knowledge she didn't dare share with the rest of the world. It made his teeth ache and his stomach queasy. He told himself it was the pocketful of candy and large coffee he'd downed on the way here.

"One that's been written about throughout the ages." Phelan ran a finger reverently along the edge of the display case. "This one is just a reproduction, but the original statue is part of a whole that has been reported to have changed the course of history."

Holt was still occupied with interviewing the estate's head butler. Brandon knew it would be some time before he was finished with the talkative older man. He let the new mystery and the increasingly intriguing woman at his side have his attention.

God, she reminded him of his fifth grade teacher, Ms. Bartholomew. Prettier, but with the same critical stare that made him squirm. She had introduced herself as the curator of the present artifacts and the currently unavailable owner's personal assistant. He bet this one was a spinster, too. Too rigid and scholarly to have a life outside of academia.

Phelan gave Brandon an appraising look. He felt like he failed her evaluation for some reason. "Betrayal, loss, and love have motivated armies and entire nations through time." He watched as her eyes narrowed slightly. "You look like a man who knows about those feelings."

Unable to control the impulse, Brandon rolled his shoulders to throw off her piercing stare and her personal implications. He knew he'd always had trouble hiding hurt and disappointment, but it was unusual for a stranger to call him on it. He decided the best defense was to ignore her comment. "And this statue helped?"

"The original, yes. When it's partnered with the other pieces of the whole, it is said to have one of the most powerful forces in the universe held within it. Each individual piece has the ability to grant its finder their heart's fondest desire."

"The whole?" He glanced at the statue. Even he recognized the six-armed gold figure from his college days. "This is Karrtikeya, Hindu god of war. The Pleiadian master. I'm not sure, but if I remember my history classes right, it doesn't need more parts to be complete."

"The statue is complete, but once combined with several other similarly blessed objects, it forms an even more powerful totem. The *Estátua Amor*."

"Love totem? You're talking about magic and *love* totems." Brandon fairly snorted his disbelief. "I thought you were an academic scholar, Ms. Phelan. They don't usually put much stock in love and magic."

"No, not usually. You're right, Detective King." She touched the glass case covering the display again, her fingers caressing the smooth glass, a faraway look in her eyes. "Unless they've seen it work for themselves." Her voice took on a softer tone and her face seemed less sharp and formal. "Everyone wants to be loved."

"Have you?" Color rose in her tanned cheeks and Brandon realized she might have misinterpreted his question as a personal one. "Seen it work, I mean?"

Phelan drew a deep breath and let it out slowly. "Let's just say my employer thinks it's worth a small fortune to have the original found."

She looked Brandon over from head to toe and smiled faintly. A slight tip of her head, a half-lidded, slanted glance out the side edge of her glasses, and a flash of something Brandon couldn't put a name to gave the woman an eerie air that made the hair on the back of his neck stand up. Gooseflesh crawled over his skin.

"Karttikeya was a warrior, much like you are. Maybe you'd like the job of finding him." She latched onto Brandon's startled gaze and held it, and him, immobile with the sheer force of her stare. "Tell me, Detective, do you already have your heart's fondest desire? Would you be willing to take a little journey and undergo a test of intelligence and stamina to earn it?"

"I'm fine, thanks." He knew he'd paused too long, stumbled over too many of his words, swallowed too hard before answering to fool her. Lord, the woman *was* just like his fifth grade teacher, reading his every thought and emotion with a glance. His subconscious put a pointed black hat on her and a bubbling cauldron at her side.

Christ, he needed to find Holt and focus on the stolen statue, not some mythical piece with magical powers.

This wasn't the reason the police had been called. The missing artifact was a piece of jade sculpture from a collection of ancient Chinese figurines no bigger than Brandon's hand. The sculpture had been out of its secure display case being readied, along with a number of other artifacts, for display during a meeting of an archaeological society at the estate this afternoon. Only one piece had disappeared. Brandon suspected it had walked out in the pocket of one of the many temporary staff that had populated the estate during the morning efforts to set up a luncheon.

Even now, dozens of black-tie adorned staff bustled about the mansion's halls and grounds preparing for the event. Smack in the middle of the activity stood his partner, designer suit, manicure, and winning smile in place. Holt looked as comfortable here as Brandon felt uneasy, which was a lot.

"Excuse me, Ms. Phelan." Brandon backed off a step. "Thanks for the lesson in myths and legends, but I think I'd better concentrate on the statue that was actually stolen."

With a curt nod, Brandon turned away, finding it hard not to glance one last time at the replica of an object that had the fabled power to fix the growing problems with his life. If his lover would only love him as much as he loved Phil, everything would work out. He knew it. But myths and legends weren't going to do that for him, no matter how persuasive the witchy woman staring him down was.

He added a cackle to his mental image of her when she gripped his arm as he stepped away. "If you find out being 'fine' isn't good enough, Detective King, you're welcome to reconsider my offer, anytime, day or night. You're intelligent, fit, and brave. You've got the perfect *heart* for the job."

"Ah, thanks. But I'm good. Really." He moved forward and her long-fingered hand dropped away, the surprisingly firm grip now nothing more than a gentle touch that slid off his arm as quickly as it had appeared.

Her only response was a small tilt of her head and a raised eyebrow that Brandon read as disbelief. The real bitch of it was, she was right. He wasn't "fine" or "good" and the thought of having his fondest desire was highly enticing. Audra Phelan was one spooky broad in his book.

He couldn't rejoin Holt fast enough in the task of spending endless hours asking pointless questions of dozens of clueless people, all of whom had seen nothing. A mouthful of pocket candies later, he felt better. There was comfort in a familiar routine, even among strangers. He wished someone would offer him coffee.

◊ ◊ ◊ ◊ ◊

The burglary investigation and interviews at the sprawling estate called Wisteria Hills took hours and the writing and filing of the report took the rest of the day. By six that evening, Brandon was tired, hungry, and craving coffee that didn't taste like it had been run through used gym socks instead of a filter.

Holt had finished his part of the report twenty minutes ago and wandered off, claiming a need to use the men's room, but Brandon watched him make a beeline to an unattended desk to pilfer an apple. He was just returning as Brandon placed the last of his paperwork into the mounting stack in his out-box.

Holt dropped onto his desk chair and slumped back, happily munching the last of his ill-gotten gains. He tossed the core into the wastebasket and leaned back, fingers laced together on his stomach and just sat. Sat and stared at Brandon.

When the silence became oppressive, Brandon glanced up from rummaging in his drawer for the last of the candies. Holt was never silent for long or without a reason. He found the other man studying him.

"What?" Brandon ate the last of the little orbs of sour-flavored sugar and waited, desperately wanting to leave Holt and the day behind him, but forced by some unseen power to stay and watch the coming disaster. Like spectators slowing after an accident, it was too compelling. Holt's earlier comments had struck more than a few nerves for him. He needed to know what more the man had perceived.

"What already? Just say it."

With a noncommittal shrug, Holt pinched his lower lip between his thumb and forefinger, a prelude to a serious comment. Brandon had seen the gesture before from watching the interaction between Holt and his vacationing partner. He knew the man was deciding whether or not to open his mouth and say something that might not be well-received.

With a sudden flash of raised eyebrows, Holt made up his mind. He started with a sigh. "You looked preoccupied all day, like your mind was on something or someone all day. Like running off while we were interviewing people to stare at that wall of sparkly artifacts with Professor Phelan."

Avoiding the implied question, Brandon ruefully muttered, "She's a curator and a personal assistant, not a professor."

"Whatever." Holt dismissed the defense. "You've still been acting...I don't know...wounded." He steepled his fingers, dropping his gaze down to stare at them as he quietly asked, "Thinking about having to be best man at your partner's wedding?"

Brandon froze in the act of chewing, then swallowed hard, a ball of ice abruptly lodged in the pit of his stomach, pushing his heart against his spine and squeezing the air from his lungs. There was a new nightmare he hadn't even thought of yet.

He rolled several candies in his fist, making them rattle, the sound filling the pregnant pause. "I've had a headache. I must be coming down with something."

All around them the usual noise and commotion of the bullpen continued. Other officers walked by, waved, or ignored the two men. Mark Edwards, one of the more talkative detectives, entered the room and started working his way toward Brandon's desk, one conversation at a time. Brandon hoped the man took his time and was all chatted out before he made it to them.

Brandon waited until Holt's gaze slowly drifted up to meet his before giving the man a small grimace and a shrug, letting Holt know he understood the real question, but that he wasn't ready to discuss it.

With a wry twist of his lips and a slow nod, Holt moved on. "If you ate something besides candy and coffee, maybe you'd feel better."

Relief surged through him. Brandon shrugged again and tossed the empty candy bag in the wastebasket. "Probably, but the drop in blood sugar would kill me."

"Want to grab a sandwich at the Grille before heading home? You really could stand to eat something decent. Caffeine and sugar won't get you far on a daily basis."

Edwards arrived at Brandon's desk. Uninvited, he leaned his oversized hip and wrinkled trousers against it, one hand searching in the open desk drawer for candy. Brandon snapped the drawer shut, barely missing Edwards's groping fingers.

Ignoring Edwards, Brandon frowned at Holt's suggestion and shook his head. "I don't know. It's late."

Edwards snickered and kicked the bottom of Holt's chair lightly. "Hey, Gregg. I see you're junior's new partner this week. You his mother now, too?"

"No, I'll let you keep on being the only *mother* in the pen, Edwards." Holt gave Edwards a toothy smile and let the implication of his true meaning cut straight to the man's jugular. "Don't you have someplace *else* to be?"

With a snort, Edwards waved away the insult. "Smartass. I'm waiting for Mike. He's in the can. I stopped by to see how all the new changes are working out for you two, that's all."

"Changes? What are you talking about?" Holt frowned and exchanged a perplexed glance with Brandon. "Our working together--" He waved a hand between himself and Brandon. "--

while not unpleasant, is only temporary. Everyone knows Briggs and Gates are on vacation."

"This week, yeah. But what about next week when Gates makes the move uptown to Homicide? He's not even coming back here from vacation to say good-bye."

"Are you sure?" Holt flashed a concerned look at Brandon, but Brandon was so floored, he couldn't even react to the news.

"Oh, yeah, real sure. Hastings up in Transfers told me. He'd know; he does the paperwork. Gates wanted it kept a secret for some reason, until he was up in Homicide, but since he's gone and never coming back, what's the big deal?" Edwards shook his head, resentment gleaming in his eyes. "Bet his fiancée had something to do with it. She's got pull in places you and I can only dream about, my friends."

He pushed off the desk and adjusted his sagging belt over a protruding belly. "You two looked so comfortable together, I thought you might be partnered up permanently. You never know, maybe Briggs will be moving on, too." He touched two fingers to his temple and gave them a jerky salute, then trudged away, mouth running before he even got close to his next unsuspecting verbal victim.

Time seemed to stand still for Brandon. The people in the room still moved about and their lips formed words, but it was all in silent slow motion for him. The knot of ice in his stomach churned, spreading its fiery chill up into his chest and blocking his throat. His lungs froze and he forgot to breathe. His worst nightmare had already come true and he'd missed it happening. Phil had left him behind without even a good-bye kiss or a so-long fuck. Then again, maybe that was what this morning had been all about. One for the road. A heavy hand on his shoulder shook him hard and the world snapped back into real time focus.

Looking up, Brandon blinked back the tears that had gathered and quickly dropped his gaze from Holt's painfully sympathetic expression. He shifted back in the chair to disengage the man's comforting touch and abruptly stood up.

"I think I'll pass on the Grille. Maybe another time. I'm..." He choked back a ball that had lodged in his throat, acid rising from his stomach, burning his words as they tumbled out. "Headache. I'm going to get some sleep."

Holt sniffed, took a long, slow breath and let it out before looking away for a second. "If you need someone to talk to--" He smiled a little. "--call me. I'll put my wife on the phone. She's the next best thing to Ann Landers."

Despite the sensation his whole life was fraying apart at the seams, Brandon huffed a dry, mirthless chuckle and nodded. "Thanks, Gregg. It's been an...interesting day."

He turned and walked out, fighting the urge to run from the building. After all, he didn't have anyone to run to. He didn't hear Holt shout, "Don't do anything stupid, hear me?" even if half the department heard.

◊ ◊ ◊ ◊ ◊

He'd been wrong. Maybe he did have someone to go to for help. He just couldn't believe Phil was going to abandon him without a word or, worse yet, expect him to be a lover on the side after Phil and Susan married. His heart wouldn't let either one of those options be real, but his brain knew better. The nagging suspicion that if he didn't do something drastic right now, before Phil returned from his trip with Susan, he would lose the man he loved for sure. He was damned if he was going to lose out to her family's money.

He loved Phil, plain and simple. Plus, the thought of starting a relationship again with someone new terrified him. He'd always picked losers. For a cop, he was surprisingly bad at sensing a man's shortcomings before he was dating him. He had both the physical and emotional scars to prove it. Phil Gates was the closest Brandon had come to finding a comfortable, semi-normal relationship. The thought of losing that relationship was almost intolerable.

Once he got into his car and started driving, his subconscious took over. Time was a blur. When it settled back to normal, Brandon found himself standing at the front door to Wisteria Hills. He had very little recall of how he got there. It had been tough driving through the -- mostly -- unshed tears. Despite the hour, the guard at the gate let him in without question, as if he had been expecting him.

As crazy as it sounded, he couldn't stop thinking about what Audra Phelan had offered -- a chance to obtain his heart's desire. The whole thing had the trappings of a fairy tale -- magical powers and love totems, things that defied logic and reason. But if he was going to salvage his crumbing relationship with Phil, he'd need a miracle and Audra Phelan was the only person offering one.

That single thread of reasoning pushed every other concern out of his mind. All around him the sounds of the night -- crickets chirping, the rustle of the leaves in the breeze -- they all seemed muted, as if paying homage to the seriousness of the occasion.

Slightly unnerved by the unnatural calm, Brandon shook the feeling off, straightened his shoulders, drew in a deep breath, and rang the doorbell. He could hear the faint bong of the bell like an ancient Chinese gong being struck. It sounded ominous and unusually powerful in the stillness of the night.

It took less than thirty seconds for the door to be answered, but Brandon had to suppress the urge to turn and run twice before the butler solemnly greeted him. He was led into a sitting room while the other man announced he would alert Ms. Phelan to Brandon's presence without Brandon even having to ask for the woman. Like the guard at the gate, the butler didn't appear surprised Brandon was back.

If he felt unnerved outside, being in the darkly furnished room, under subdued lighting, in the very still, massive house was even more disquieting to Brandon. All sound in the house was muted, an effect of the thick carpeting and the tapestry on the walls. The manservant's feet hadn't even made a sound as he moved in and out of the banquet-sized room. Brandon had the urge to break one of the fine Oriental porcelain urns on a side table just to hear a noise other than the pounding of his heart against his rib cage.

Too anxious to sit, Brandon fidgeted in place for a bit, studying the oil paintings on the walls. Studying turned into fingering the many intricate objects on the polished mahogany tables. As he worked his way deeper into the room, he realized it was the same interview room he and Holt had used that morning, now nearly unrecognizable in the dim light and growing shadows of the evening.

Knowing the Karttikeya statue's display case was here, Brandon moved deeper into the room until he found the correct alcove. Without illumination from within, the glass front of the case was opaque, its transparent surface a smoky black that showed Brandon only his reflection instead of the statue he was desperately longing to see again.

He knew it was there. He could feel it, a tangible aura that pulled at him, compelling him to come closer. He didn't know if it was this statue or the others in the collection that drew him. Ms. Phelan had implied that the Karttikeya statue was the last that needed to be collected, so the others must be the real deal.

Brandon reached out to tentatively touch the glass, imagining the coveted golden statue. The moment his hand met the smooth, cool surface, a spark of electricity rippled along his fingertips and up his arm. He felt a rush of excitement constrict his chest, followed by a flash of warmth that flooded his entire body and seeped into the deep recesses of his mind, touching parts of his soul he couldn't reveal to anyone. It was beautiful and comforting, but Brandon found it frightening at the same time. He jerked his hands back, rubbing the fingertips over his palm to lessen the lingering burn in them. He wished he'd bought another bag of candies after work. He could use the sugar rush to calm his nerves right about now. That or a big cup of good coffee would work, too.

The display backlights inexplicably jumped to life and he stumbled back a step in surprise.

"Does this help, Detective King?" Ms. Phelan's cultured, crisp tone sent a shiver up Brandon's spine. He could feel a guilty flush creep up his face.

"Yes, thank you. It does." He dragged his imagination back under control and turned to face the woman, hoping she'd miss or ignore the bright color in his cheeks. The stutter didn't help any. "I wanted...I thought.... I've been wondering about the statue. I needed a second look at it."

Phelan came to stand at his side, her gaze locked on his face while he turned to stare into the display case. He searched for something ominous and unusual among the artifacts, but all he could see was a grouping of old, beautiful, artistic oddities. None glowed a ghostly white nor grew new arms or eyes while he watched. But the power was still there, radiating from behind the glass, calling to him, almost like a physical caress to his aching soul. He tried to chalk up the spark he still felt in his hand to static electricity in the carpet, but the tingle increased as he stared at the display, making him rub his fingertips with his thumb to try to quiet the sensation. It didn't work.

"Thinking of taking me up on my offer?"

The room seemed smaller somehow, quieter and less overwhelming when the woman used a softer tone of voice. Brandon relaxed, letting his need show just a tiny bit.

"How did you know I'd be back?" He glanced at her face, reassured by her understanding expression. The lack of a smile helped in this case. At least she wasn't mocking him or his feelings. "Or that I was interested in the first place?"

She shrugged and her eyelids fluttered as if they were beating back a memory, keeping it from showing in her eyes. It reached her voice despite her efforts. "I know something about being denied our heart's fondest desire. Enough to recognize it in others."

"Does it really have the ability to grant love?"

"Can't you feel the power now? If you need affirmation, step closer to them."

Her stare wasn't accusatory, but Brandon grew restless under the intensity of it. He stepped closer to the glass and the edge of his discomfort faded away. He flashed her a look full of disbelief, but Phelan's expression never changed.

"Amazing, is it not? The power to heal and soothe a wounded heart." There was an element of awe in her voice that was infectious. Brandon looked at the objects with a growing respect. "What you feel is the force of the individual artifacts. The parts that make up the final totem, but each has its own ability to grant true love." She nodded at the small, glistening Hindu god astride the peacock. "Retrieve the original statue of Karttikeya, Detective King, and return it to this collection and your fondest heart's desire will be yours for all time."

"What will happen to it once you have it? What do you get out of this?"

This all sounded too fantastic to be true, but Brandon could feel the power emanating from behind the glass. The closer he got to it, the more gooseflesh broke out on his arms. He touched the glass a second time, wanting to ask her about the sparkle and snap of electric current he'd experienced last time, but now instead of a shock, a vague feeling of contentment embraced him. It was a nice change from the worry and pain he'd been carrying around all day, but was it real? Was anything here to be taken seriously?

"A complete, priceless, ancient totem that hasn't been reassembled in centuries. A valuable prize for any archaeologist, wouldn't you say, Detective? Worth the cost and the wait."

"Wait?"

Phelan's gaze traveled over each artifact, lingering on one, then another piece, eyes studying each unique item as if it were the first time she had seen them.

"The totem picks the finder of its pieces. That takes time. It attracts only those who need it and pulls them to it." She glanced at Brandon. "It's not coincidence that you're the one who came to investigate today. The totem chose you."

Brandon snorted in disbelief but Ms. Phelan merely shrugged. "Our local police told me it's been years since they needed to transfer a case to another station. But today they did need to. Today, you were the detective that got handed the case." She looked Brandon over once, eyes kinder and voice gentler. "And today is the day you found out you need more than just a loving heart to have your dreams come true, didn't you?"

A ball caught in the back of Brandon's throat and he couldn't do more than swallow around it and jerk his head in a fitful nod of embarrassment until the lump shrunk enough for him to speak. "How did you know?"

God, what he wouldn't give for a quart of coffee right now. Something to wash away the acid burn of shame.

She shook her head, her neatly arranged hair capturing the light from the display case, making her suddenly look vulnerable, less rigid, than she had a moment ago. "The totem knew. Its power is growing, the more complete it becomes. You are the twelfth and final lover to be called to it. You need it. It needs you. A fairly simple arrangement."

"Why me? There must be a lot of people around who would love to have their heart's desire granted."

"You have abilities and traits that will be needed to find the last piece. The totem always chooses wisely. Not everyone deserves to have his or her heart's desire. We've learned to trust it over the years."

"We?"

"My employer and I."

"Ah. The true collector of all these objects. Your employer must be a very rich person to afford to fund hunts for all these things." He looked over the eclectic array of objects and wondered where each one had been found and what it had taken to get them back to this protective glass sanctuary. He wondered if it had been worth the cost to the people involved and what he'd end up paying for the privilege when it was all over. Nothing was free or easy. He'd learned that early in life.

The idea of having Phil all for himself, of truly being happy for once, was worth just about any price right now.

"What's the deal include?"

Ms. Phelan turned her back on the display and moved a few feet away from it, her voice all business again. "We will provide you with all the information we've gathered as to the statue's last recorded whereabouts. We'll point you in the right direction, fully fund every aspect of your travel to retrieve the statue, and guarantee your old life will be waiting for you when you return." She paused, then added, "That is, if you still want it then."

"*If* I want my life back?" He couldn't stop the disbelief from showing. "Why do you think I'd do this if I didn't want to come back?"

"Detective King, you're searching for a different life after all, aren't you? One that includes true love? You wouldn't be here if you were happy with the life you have now. Many find out that their fondest desire actually has nothing to do with what they *think* they want."

Brandon wanted to argue with her, but something in her gaze told him she was more right than he would like her to be. "I'll keep that in mind."

With one last glance at the smiling statue of Karttikeya, he turned away to focus on what the woman could tell him. "What kind of information do you have? I'm... not sure how much time I have to accomplish this in."

"You have time, Detective. Trust me, and if not, trust the totem."

CHAPTER FOUR

The antiquities shop looked like every other little storefront along the colorful, busy marketplace. It was a bit worn, the paint starting to fade and the front picture window a little dusty and smudged with fingerprints. The once dark green canopy over the open doorway was a paler shade of moss, frayed at the edges. The building showed the signs of either neglect or a shop owner too busy to notice the wear and tear.

Unable to decide which from the sidewalk, Brandon stepped through the open doorway and down two steps into the store. The temperature immediately dropped ten degrees. Brandon shook off a little shiver as it scurried down his spine.

Cautious of the numerous shapes and tables around him, Brandon fumbled his way deeper into the coolness of the store, vision momentarily cloaked in gray shadows and blurry outlines as it adjusted to the extreme change from brilliant sunlight to relative sudden darkness.

Once his eyesight cleared, he became fascinated by the structured chaos around him. Everywhere he looked a broken clay pot, a chipped porcelain plate, or some other seemingly ancient piece of some supposed long-forgotten culture stood on display. He remembered enough from his college days to know these were real, but probably not very valuable, pieces of history.

Many were from the Native American tribes, but he thought the masks and stone figures belonged to the rain forest cultures, primitive and beautiful in their raw, artistic states. It had been a long time since he'd called on those few ancient civilization courses he'd indulged in before deciding on a career in law enforcement. He didn't regret his decision to become a cop, but occasionally he found he missed having friends who talked about something more involved than shooting range scores, football scores, and just plain scoring.

"Hello? Anybody?"

The store appeared empty of other human life, no shopkeeper or cashier manning the glass-topped service counter or the large, old, brass cash register. He reached out to touch several wonderful, but delicate-looking, pieces, but resisted the urge at the last moment. Brandon carefully wove his way through the maze of tables piled with artifacts, tools, and old books. On the counter lay a pile of posted letters and mailed business fliers, with one large manila envelope layered between the white edges and stamped corners. It looked like any ordinary business envelope, but it registered with his detective mind. Brandon had one like it folded and stuffed into his back pocket.

He glanced on the floor behind the counter, naturally suspicious of possible foul play in an unattended store. Finding nothing but crates of partially unpacked items, he started a stealthy walk toward a drapery-covered doorway in the back.

"Hello? Anyone here?"

Brandon started when a husky, rich voice answered out of the shadows off to his left.

"Good morning." A man stepped out of the gloom and Brandon wondered why he hadn't seen him the moment his eyesight had adjusted. Even among the hundreds of objects, tall cabinets, and stacked tables, this man stood out like a wet dream.

He was at least six foot two, tall compared to Brandon's slight, five foot ten inch, one hundred sixty-pound frame. The man was at least two hundred twenty pounds and all of it, from what Brandon could see, was toned, tanned, and rippling under the snug, gray denim work shirt and faded blue jeans, which molded to firm, muscular thighs. Even the scuffed brown moccasins on his feet were sexy.

His black hair fell in waves to his collar and the V of chest hairs visible between the edges of the open neck of the shirt were the same rich color, moderately thick and just as curly. His eyes were a pale shade of gray flecked with threads of black that made them look like polished marble.

Right now those eyes, combined with a sultry smile on full, parted lips, held an expression Brandon read as somewhere between attraction and amusement. Both made him feel a little uncomfortable, each for a different reason.

"Sorry. I didn't realize you were there. Didn't see you when I came in." He felt a tingle of warmth at his cheekbones. "You know, bright sunlight to dark shop. It threw me off."

"I should have said something. I was enjoying watching you explore my shop. I like it when a person knows enough about what he's looking at to appreciate and respect it." He gave Brandon a head to toe appraising look that took longer than politely acceptable. "You'd be surprised how many try to handle precious things like they're cheap clutter off their grandmother's mantel. You're not one of those." The man stuck out his hand in greeting. "I'm Christian Carter, part-time shop owner, full-time archaeologist, and occasional chief procurer of artifacts and antiquities."

"Brandon King."

They shook hands, Christian's grip a little firmer than it needed to be. It lasted a bit longer than necessary, too. The smile on his handsome face was playful and engaging enough that Brandon found himself returning the pressure, and even let his fingers trail over the man's palm as their hands fell away. A tingle of pleasure warmed his fingertips.

"What can I help you with, Brandon King? A gift for a history lover or maybe... just for a lover?" He smiled and cocked his head to one side, his question somehow made more intimate by the small gesture. "What's her taste run to? Ancient Chinese or southwestern Native American? I can show you some lovely pieces from both cultures."

"My lover wouldn't know an ancient Chinese urn from a department store knickknack." Recognizing the probing question for what it was, Brandon smiled back at Christian and gave him what he was looking for. "Intriguing history for *him* is last week's hockey scores."

"Ah. Well. He's missing out on a lot of great...adventures." Christian winked at Brandon, putting more husky emphasis on his last word and changing the entire meaning of it in that instant. He relaxed his stance, hands spread wide on his hips, an openly teasing expression on his tan, chiseled face.

"Exploring the unknown and discovering new things can be a very..." His gaze wandered over Brandon's face and down his body before coming back up to stare into Brandon's eyes. "...satisfying and enjoyable experience."

Flattered and slightly off balance at the overt attention, Brandon gave a dry chuckle. "I'll bet you say that to all your customers."

"Only the handsome, exciting ones." Christian's gaze became intense, full of desire, a blatant, but charming, invitation to more. Phil was pretty good at saying the right things at times, but he didn't have the casual charm and sincerity Christian did.

A thrill ran through Brandon, turning his palms sweaty and heightening the warmth in his cheeks. He felt his own jeans grow snug as his dick responded to the sensual implication of Christian's come-on. It had been a long time since he felt immediate chemistry with anyone like this. Not even Phil had made his cock jump at their first handshake.

Brandon especially liked the sharp angle of Christian's cheekbones. It gave the man's appearance a bold strength that made Brandon want to taste the bronzed skin caressing the planes of his square jaw and dusky rose lips.

A phone behind the counter rang, breaking the moment.

Brandon laughed, nervous and uncertain as to what reply he should make. It sure as hell couldn't be the reply he was thinking of. He doubted *"Let me lick your lips until the color comes off"* could be interpreted as a mildly friendly gesture. He couldn't believe he was standing here thinking these things when he had come to this man to help him find a way to keep Phil at his side.

"Hang on a minute, okay?" Christian didn't move toward the insistent ringing until Brandon nodded his agreement.

He wandered around the shop, glancing into corners and inspecting items big and small, anything that piqued his interest. Nine times out of ten it was something so bizarre he didn't have any clue what it was and his cop's instincts clamored to be satisfied with a full investigation. In this shop, he figured it would take him a lifetime to check out all the unknowns. It was a pity he wasn't going to be around longer. This shop, and its owner, would be very attractive to spend some of his off-hours exploring. The thought made his already firm dick jump, increasing the delicious pressure inside his pants.

For the third time since he'd entered the shop, his hand wandered to his jacket pocket looking for candy that wasn't there. He should have hit the twenty-four hour convenience store for coffee and a bag of the needed sweets before he came. He made a mental reminder not to be in such a big hurry that his nutritional needs suffered. Not that sugar and caffeine counted as nutrition, but it was all he felt like stomaching for the last day and a half.

Emotional stress ate at Brandon like the cancer that had taken away his mother and chased his father away from his mother's side when she got sick. He could lose Phil. It would eat him alive just like a disease. He didn't want to be alone again and he didn't have the energy to start a new relationship. Even promising moments like this one with Christian would end up nothing more than a one-night stand if he let it get out of hand. Experience had taught him men as attractive and self-confident as this man didn't stay interested in Brandon for long. Cops who didn't like to use their cuffs at home in the bedroom, read books besides police manuals, preferred the theater over the football field, and men over women, were doomed to spend a lot of nights doing those things by themselves. It would be better if he just concentrated on business and forgot about the thrill that Christian's heated glance gave him.

Taking advantage of Christian being distracted on the phone, Brandon used the moment to subtly rearrange himself in his jeans, trying to will his swelling cock back down to a less noticeable bulge. It would make thinking easier, too. Brandon needed to focus on the job he came here to do and fantasizing about Christian while yearning for Phil didn't make sense.

The materials Ms. Phelan had given him before he left the estate were tucked into his back pocket. It included special travel visas, photos of the original Karttikeya statue believed to belong to the totem, the figurine's last known whereabouts, and a literary journal article on myths surrounding it. Some of it was daunting, and a good potion of it Brandon just flat out disbelieved, dismissing it as impossible. But it was also intriguing. Compelling on a level Brandon hadn't ever experienced before. He felt exhilarated by the idea of an adventure to a foreign country to rediscover a long lost artifact with legendary powers.

It was like playing the part of Indiana Jones. He felt as if he had been given permission to be reckless, free from his usual rules and restraints. He was almost as anxious to start the quest for the sake of the adventure as for the prize at the end of the rainbow.

He had the athletic skills and marksmanship abilities to play the role, but he felt a huge deficiency on the archaeological end of the knowledge scale, which he suspected he'd need for this quest. The statue was cloaked in so much mystery and myth, he could see a need for the knowledge of these things playing a part in its recovery. And that was why he was here.

He turned back to glance at Christian just as he was hanging up the phone.

Christian came back to stand with Brandon, the manila envelope from the mail stack on the countertop in his hands. He wore a thoughtful, mildly guarded look, his gray eyes serious, but his gaze just as heated and intense as before. Maybe more so.

"That was an unusual conversation. One-sided, really."

"Yeah?" Surprised, but only mildly interested, Brandon shoved his hands into his empty jacket pockets to keep them off a particularly compelling display piece, and silently bemoaned the lack of sugar pebbles that should have been in them.

"It was from an anonymous caller." Christian's gaze turned more intense and Brandon fought the urge to squirm under it. "It was about you." He hefted the manila envelope in his hand. "And this." He flipped the envelope over so that the precise handwriting on the front was visible to Brandon. "It came with the morning mail, but I just noticed it doesn't have any postage on it."

Brandon frowned and squinted up at Christian, one hand reaching out and taking the envelope to examine it. "What about me? What did the caller say?" The back flap was still sealed and a wide piece of packing tape had been affixed over the edges, doubly securing it.

"To look in the envelope." He frowned slightly, but his eyes held the glint of increased interest when he looked at Brandon. "And if you didn't show up here to look for you. *Detective.*"

"I'm on personal time." He managed not to sound defensive. He didn't like people knowing he was a cop unless they needed to know. People tended to keep him at a distance once they knew and he really didn't want this man to back away. He handed the package back to Christian. "You haven't opened it yet."

"No, I haven't." Christian glanced at the envelope, but let his stare settle on Brandon's face. "Why don't you tell me what this is all about first?"

A deep breath and long exhalation didn't seem to make the whole thing make any more sense than it did before he walked into the shop. "Listen. It's a long story and some of it even I don't believe, but basically, I came here for information. Facts, clues, stories, suggestions -- anything that can help me find a certain artifact and get it back here intact. That's why I came to you. To talk to someone who knows about this piece. Knows more than just its history."

"Why to me? There are other more academic-minded people experienced in archaeology around here."

"Maybe, but not like you." Brandon was surprised at the awe in his own voice. He hadn't given much time to examining it, but Christian Carter had made a very distinguished name for himself. Looking at him in the flesh, Brandon thought the legend fit the man.

"I researched it for over seven hours at the university library. Your name kept coming up – in articles, journals, papers, not just about your knowledge on the subject or as a field archaeologist, but about your skill as an explorer. You work as an acquiring agent for a lot of museums." Brandon spread his hands out in front of him as he talked, working them into loose fists, then opening them again as if he was trying to grasp or hold onto something that eluded him time and time again. "I need to talk to someone who has been to the jungles in India. Who has done what I'm looking to do." He swallowed hard and fought down the sensation of despair that the thought of failing, of losing Phil, created in his gut.

"I *need* to succeed. I don't have time to waste on figuring it all out myself. I need someone who can give me some advice on how to do it." He studied Christian's face, taking in his sharp gaze, his strong, muscle-wrapped frame, and the intelligent gleam in his marble eyes. "I'm asking for your help. Some guidance, a few suggestions. I have maps, instructions on how to get part of the way to where I need to be. Even guides and supplies are waiting for me, but I need to know more about what I'm looking for."

"What are you looking for?" Christian's demeanor hardened, suddenly the seasoned explorer and protector of the bits and pieces of history around them.

"A small golden statue of the Hindu god Karttikeya riding a peacock."

"Why?" His tone was clipped, a suspicious edge to it.

"Someone is paying me to get it." Falling into detective mode, Brandon voiced only the bare minimum of facts.

Christian's stern gaze never wavered and Brandon knew he'd have to give up more than mere monetary gain to convince the man to help. He needed something to grab his professional interest without making Brandon sound like a foolish schoolgirl looking for a magic love potion.

"But I'm not doing it for the money. It's part of a collection, a totem. The benefit I get out of it is...in the finding of it." That wasn't completely untrue. The idea of the adventure had started to appeal to Brandon.

There was a long pause as Christian stared at Brandon and chewed the inside of his lower lip, a move Brandon found erotic and very distracting. "You're talking about the *Estátua Amor.*"

"You know of it?" Brandon paced a little in place, antsy and craving a cup of coffee. He'd need a double espresso soon just to get through the remainder of the morning.

"Every archaeologist knows of it. It's legendary. No one's seen it for over nine hundred years. I've been hunting for the pieces of it for the last five years. I arranged for the purchase of a few of the pieces for an anonymous collector a couple of years ago, but never obtained one myself. If that's what you're looking for, finding it won't be easy."

"I'm not looking for or expecting easy. That's why I need to be prepared. 'Knowledge is power,' and all that."

"Where you headed?"

"India. Supposedly the statue was last seen in the main chamber of an abandoned temple deep in the jungle north of Madhya Pradesh." His tongue tripped a little over the name but he knew he'd said it well enough.

Recognition put a gleam of excitement in Christian's eyes and a speculative look on his face. "The Lost Temple of Karttikeya." He tucked the envelope under his arm as he folded them over his chest, arm muscles straining the fabric of his shirtsleeves, drawing Brandon's attention.

"The temple is reported to be in the heart of the jungle north of Bhopāl, near the Chambal River. You'll need more than a few pointers to get there, Detective. It's about as far away from civilization as anyone should get." Christian's face clouded over with concern, his gaze reassessing Brandon anew with every slow blink of his eyelids. "You might want to reconsider."

"I need to go." Brandon hadn't meant for the words to come out so husky and needy, but they did and he couldn't pull them back. His mind reeled with all the details the trip involved, but at the moment he had to take care of immediate needs first. "I also need a cup of coffee. Is there anyplace here where I could get some?"

"Then I'd love to take you." Christian grinned and cocked an eyebrow up. A flush of warmth filled Brandon's chest and his jeans before Christian added, "To the coffee shop, at least. Then we can talk some more about the temple. What's your boyfriend think about all this?" He followed an eager Brandon toward the door.

It took Brandon a moment to think of a vague answer, but he knew the hurt in his voice gave away the truth. "He's currently seeing other people."

"Ah."

That single syllable cut Brandon to the quick. He felt like his whole pathetic love life had just been laid out in the open. He took a calming breath and waited for the inevitable cutting remark.

Christian Carter had probably never known the pain of losing a lover or of facing a lifetime alone. Men who looked like he did never had shitty affairs and lonely nights. Handsome, built, intelligent, and successful with an exciting career. Who the hell would want to leave that behind?

"Then maybe this *is* my lucky day." Christian grinned and winked, slipping one hand on the small of Brandon's back under his jacket to guide him out the door.

Brandon was stunned into letting him, the sudden, surprising warmth on his spine and the delighted tone in Christian's husky voice shocking him into a compliant silence. It was almost enough to make him forget he needed coffee. Almost.

◊ ◊ ◊ ◊ ◊

Midmorning sunlight cast a warm glow through the French door glass, sending rainbows of color to dance on the slate floor by the doors. Audra Phelan moved closer to the wheelchair sitting in the band of light and knelt beside it.

"Detective King has made contact with Carter." Her hands automatically tucked the lap blanket deeper down the side of the chair, pulling it snugly around the legs of the chair's occupant. Once the job was completed, she let her hand rest on the man's knee, her fingers affectionately rubbing over the loose weave. "I wonder if they'll hit it off." She placed her arm on the side bar of the chair and propped her chin on it to look into the man's face.

A weary grunt came from the man in the wheelchair, his voice weak and the lines in his face seemingly deeper to her than they had been yesterday. "But will they have time to retrieve the statue is the real question."

"They'll find it, Andrew." Her fingers gripped his knee reassuringly, then relaxed. "We have time."

Andrew Martin, famed archaeologist and lifelong collector of priceless oddities and antiquities, caressed her cheek and smiled at her. "If you say so, Audra. I trust your judgment. You haven't failed me yet."

She smiled back, her hand coming off his knee to lace fingers with his at her cheek. He was fast becoming one of his own ancient artifacts, frail and brittle with the passing of time. Audra hoped they *did* have the time she was professing existed.

She had been Andrew's assistant for over thirty-five years. They had spent a lifetime together. She was determined Andrew would have his chance at his lifelong dream, his own heart's desire. And Brandon King was going to help accomplish that goal.

And if she had done her job right, Christian Carter was going to help him. Andrew could no longer travel to the ends of the earth and fight at the gates of hell, but those two men could and would in his place.

CHAPTER FIVE

Coffee turned into lunch and a brainstorming session, which lasted into late afternoon. Brandon had been too keyed up to eat, anxious to start the adventure, but he found he enjoyed Christian's company too much to object to the loss of time. The dread that had been lodged in the pit of his gut since he realized Phil was planning on marrying Susan thawed a little under the warmth of Christian's smile and teasing innuendo.

"It's nice to sit here and have coffee, and not worry about who sees us or what they'll think."

"Your boyfriend doesn't take you out?"

Contemplating how much he wanted Christian to know about his personal life, Brandon paused before deciding he needed to be honest and trust the man if they were going to do this adventure together. He was never very good at keeping secrets anyway. That was part of the problem with his relationship with Phil. It felt deceitful to everyone involved.

"We're partners at work. Cops aren't the most accepting of gays in their ranks, no matter what the policies say. Phil likes to keep our off-duty relationship...quiet." In contrast to how it made Brandon feel to admit that, it was nice to be in the company of someone who didn't try to hide the fact he was attracted to him, someone who paid attention to him outside of a bedroom.

"Excuse me for saying so, but the man's a selfish ass, Brandon. I've been having a great time letting all those staring eyes around us think we're together." Christian slid his hand across the table and playfully tugged at the hem of Brandon's coat sleeve, leaving his fingers resting on the leather when he was done.

It was a small thing, but an intimate gesture nonetheless, and it sent a burst of heat through Brandon's chest that shot down to his groin. It had been ages since he'd had someone flirt with him, and it felt good. He was enjoying himself, suddenly pleased the Jet Airways tickets in his manila envelope didn't have him depart for India until the next day.

He signaled the waiter for more coffee and took a sip out of the remains in his cup so he wouldn't have to respond.

Neither one of them was completely surprised when Christian's matching envelope contained all the tickets and paperwork for him to accompany Brandon. The only thing that was added was a precisely penned note that simply read: "If you both have enough sense to use them."

The people engineering this quest had thought of everything so far, including arranging backup for Brandon. They certainly wanted this statue found. Expense was obviously no object. There were travelers' checks amounting to over twenty thousand dollars in each of their packets. Brandon didn't know whether to be thrilled with the financial freedom it offered or disheartened by the ominous idea they would need that much cash to make this trip work.

A small backpack stuffed with a few changes of socks and underwear, a fresh shirt, a toothbrush and comb, and Brandon was ready to go. A bottle of super bug repellent, a well-stocked first aid kit, and his cell phone topped off the list of necessities.

He'd taken the first two hours of the morning to visit the private doctor's office listed on the papers to get his immunizations. Immediately ushered into a small office upon arrival, the paperwork had been completed in record time. The nurse had been efficient, precise, and silent the whole time. He'd almost felt like he was a ghost during the visit, except his arms now ached and his ass burned from being used for a pincushion.

He added his own passport to the slim stack of government paperwork required to leave the country on short notice. Those joined the thicker pile of maps, instructions, and photos that was currently padding his back pocket, pressing against the painful spot on his butt cheek.

He shifted in his chair, taking the weight off his sore ass, and refocused his attention on what Christian was saying. He enjoyed watching how the man pursed his lips between sentences, and chewed on the inside of his lower lip when he was discussing something serious.

"I've had all the immunizations I need for this trip last spring. I went to Malaysia for a six-week excursion. Between the travel visas they included in the envelope and my passport, I'm good to go. I always keep a bag packed, just in case."

"You do a lot of traveling in your line of work, don't you?"

The coffee was hot and rich, with no trace of chicory in it. The Colombian beans were freshly ground and the coffeepot had been cleaned. Brandon could always tell. It was pure nectar of the gods. Eyes closed in bliss, he gulped half of his third cup down, savoring the last mouthful before letting it slide down his throat.

When he opened his eyes, he was embarrassed to find Christian watching him, eyes intense and gaze heated. It didn't help the sudden fullness in his jeans when Christian licked his bottom lip, slow and provocative. Brandon's cock jumped and swelled. A flash of guilt raced through him, but it was chased away by a shiver of pleasure that he had been able to put that look in the handsome man's eyes.

He cleared his throat, hands toying with his coffee cup and repeated his unanswered question just for something to say. "You must be gone a lot."

With an elegant shrug of his broad shoulders, Christian held his gaze locked on Brandon's face, his eyes saying more than his words did. "No reason not to be. Nobody to keep me home." He chewed the inside of his lip again. "Want to apply for the position?"

Brandon chuckled and swallowed past the ball in his throat. "Currently unavailable, remember?"

"I can wait." Christian winked and tugged lightly on Brandon's still captured sleeve. "And you should remember I'm a professional at acquiring priceless works of art."

"Well, Indiana, you'll get a chance to show how much skill you have on the trip." He was surprised by his own immediate response. Brandon blushed, but didn't take it back.

"I like the sound of that. You've got a deal, David." Those gray eyes flashed, pupils dilating slightly. At Brandon's questioning look, he added, "My favorite piece of priceless art."

"Yeah, right." Brandon snorted into his coffee to brush off the teasing compliment, but he didn't pull his sleeve away or drop his gaze. He decided the man had great eyes. They looked like marble, but they were warm and inviting, with a depth and caring he didn't ever see in Phil's eyes, even when they were making love. That thought startled him. He'd never considered the way Phil looked at him before. Never thought to compare it to the interest in anyone else's expression. Maybe he had been too wrapped up in having someone, anyone, close that he was settling for less than he could have.

But then what he could have *wouldn't* be someone like Christian Carter, no matter how much flirting the other man did. It was fun, but that's all it was. The Carters in this world were meant for others like themselves. Not short, thin, wiry, reclusive cops leading a semi-closeted life with no family and few friends. Brandon knew he wasn't unattractive, but he was more "cute and cuddly" than the "wow, look at him" type that Christian was. David he was not. That was more Christian's calling.

Even now, sitting in this coffee shop, the approving glances came their way. He downed the last of his coffee as quickly as he could and tried not to look self-conscious. It *was* nice to be out in public with a man who didn't mind them being viewed as a couple. He'd forgotten how much he'd missed the simple things like that since dating Phil. If you could call their relationship dating. It was really more of an affair, now that he thought of it. An affair, dark and dirty, just like that word implied.

Brandon chased that thought away. Once he found the statue and was granted his heart's desire, Phil would be open about their relationship. As much as he wanted to believe that, something indefinable nagged at the back of his brain, warning him. He pushed it away before it became clear, unwilling to have his hopes and dreams shaken when he was so close to obtaining them. He'd examine them once he had the statue in hand.

After all, hadn't Ms. Phelan said the totem would know what he wanted better than he did? Brandon just hoped he wouldn't be too surprised by it.

◊ ◊ ◊ ◊ ◊

The trip to India has been long, uncomfortable, and noisy. The multiple flights between airports in multiple countries and the transports between various cities had been a convoluted arrangement of bartering and cash. Thankfully, Christian was adept and experienced at negotiations. Nearly forty-eight hours after departing the USA, they finally found themselves in Bhopāl, the capital of Madhya Pradesh, and soon after that they were as near to their goal as they could get by a motorized vehicle.

As night fell on their third day out, they found themselves sharing a single room in a small hotel in a tiny village on the edge of a vast forest. The hotel room was cool, the noise from the busy, dusty main street muffled by shutters and thick throw carpets, and the linens on the bed fresh, crisp, and colorful.

Sitting on the only bed in the room, Brandon sighed at the thought of sleeping in the same bed, no matter how large, with Christian. The clerk at the desk had insisted it was the best room, and the only one available.

It was beautiful, decorated with full drapes of white mosquito netting surrounding the low queen-size bed covered with silk sheets. Dozens of jewel-toned pillows, both on the bed and the floor, gave the room a bright, exotic look. The room was cool in the shadows, a soft breeze in constant motion from the two large ceiling fans. It was more than he expected from what had appeared, from the lobby, to be a shabby little hotel.

He wasn't concerned about getting a comfortable night's sleep in an actual bed anymore. He was worried about sleeping a foot away from Christian, in the same bed, all night. He didn't think he had the kind of self-control it would take to make it through the night on his own side of the bed without embarrassing himself. He stared at the small, ancient divan at the end of the bed, wondering if he could come up with an acceptable reason to sleep on it for the night.

Over the last three days, he and Christian had spent every moment together. They laughed over simple things, like boldly sampled native cuisine, which brought searing heat to Brandon's unsuspecting taste buds and tears to his eyes. They discussed their coming adventure, then touched on their love lives – Brandon's current unsatisfying one and Christian's past relationships, their present jobs, and even future goals.

He knew more about Christian after three days than he did about Phil after several months of working and sleeping with the man. It made Brandon realize just how hollow and superficial a relationship he had with his partner. It also made him want more. More from life, more from a boyfriend, more than he knew Phil was capable of giving. He doubted that even

Susan was getting much more out of her relationship with Phil than he was.

Responding to Christian's attention and comfortable company, Brandon had relaxed his guard. He knew Christian thought Phil was using him. Christian's quiet disapproval had revealed the shame about the way he had been allowing Phil to dictate and hide their relationship. He'd managed to keep it hidden from everyone, including himself, until this trip. Until he'd found someone who made him remember what it was like to be respected and appreciated as a valued equal. Someone who enjoyed talking to him and doing everyday things with him as much as his heated, teasing gaze suggested he would enjoy touching Brandon.

His heart's desire hadn't changed; it just wore an unseen face now. He'd like to say it was Christian, but he knew better. This was just fate throwing them together for an adventure. After it was over, Christian would move on to a new chapter in his life and so would he. Christian's would just involve handsome hunks and more intriguing adventures, while the best thing he could look forward to would be a new work partner and a lonely bed in an empty apartment.

He bounced on the bed and sighed again. It was comfortable, plush, and quiet. Damn.

Falling back onto the bed, he closed his eyes, blocking out the dust particles floating in the beam of sunlight streaming through the shuttered window the way he wanted to block the ache in his chest. He'd come to realize wanting, *trying* to force Phil to love him was a waste of time that would only make them both miserable in the long run. That knowledge didn't make letting go of his dream any easier to accept.

The dull ache under his rib cage reminded him of the pain he'd felt when his mother passed away, ravaged by a fast-growing cancer, her death severing his last tie to any form of family. This didn't hurt as much as her passing had, but it still made a hole in his life. Phil had been his work partner and his bed partner. Now, without any real warning, he was gone. Brandon knew he needed to move on. He just had to figure out how. Right after he figured out how to sleep next to Christian night after night without jacking off.

That idea appealed to his lower half and his cock swelled, confined behind his jeans and tight-knit boxers. His hand automatically moved inside his pants to ease the snug fit, his palm rubbing heavily against his rapidly filling dick as it reacted to the sudden handling. Eyes still closed, Brandon's mouth fell partially open, his breath coming in shallow pants as his fingers rubbed circles over the head of his shaft, coaxing pre-cum from the tip to smear under his fingers to soothe the delicious friction he was creating. It had been days since he'd had the opportunity for a little one-handed relief, and he needed it.

Christian was downstairs making sure the guide and supplies were ready for tomorrow morning's hike into the jungle. But Brandon wasn't surprised when it was Christian's face his mind saw during his moment of self-pleasuring, or that it was Christian's hand he imagined wrapped around his shaft instead of Phil's more familiar fingers. He wasn't even surprised when Christian's smooth, sultry voice spoke to him.

"I could help you with that." The voice climbed right inside his jeans and stroked his dick right along with his hand.

"God, you already are." He picked up the pace, wishing he'd unzipped his pants before he'd started. Now he didn't want to let go long enough to do it. He moaned when his zipper slid down seemingly on its own. He spread his legs wider and tightened his grip, riding the waves of pleasure rippling up from the pit of his lower abdomen and balls. He hit the crest of the wave and took it for all it was worth, bucking up into his hand, twisting his hips, grinding his ass into the mattress, letting the small jet of cum splatter his belly from under the elastic waistband of his shorts. He couldn't stop murmuring the name of the person who had given him so much pleasure from falling off his tongue.

"Christian! Fuck!"

"We can do that." The husky voice was dark, rich with passion, and even tinged with surprise. The mattress dipped and warmth pressed along the length of his body, a solid, real hand pushed his own away to grip his shrinking cock. His dick jumped back to life at the silky, callused touch of unfamiliar fingers. A muscular leg draped over one of his own, holding Brandon in place by sheer weight, not force. "I was beginning to think you weren't as attracted to me as I am to you."

"W-what?" Brandon's eyelids flew open as his head jerked up in shock. Panic made his eyes wide, he felt color rising in his cheeks, but Christian ignored it all, sealing their mouths together in a kiss that silenced whatever further comment had been on Brandon's lips.

The kiss was harshly sweet, full of desire and need, brimming with the newness of a first touch. Brandon's mind reeled with the unexpected pleasure of it while his body responded. His mouth opening to the ravenous kiss, hips rising up to meet the heavy, skillful caress of his slick cock in warm hand. His dick jerked, going plump and firm with each stroke of Christian's hand, the lazy rhythm competing with the more rapid play of eager tongue against tongue. It was long minutes before it ended.

Breathless and excited, Brandon was still unsure. He liked Christian; he just didn't think they should cloud their working arrangement with intimacy, at least not this soon. There were so many things he wasn't completely certain about, not the least of which were his changing feelings about Phil. His growing attraction for Christian wasn't helping him think clearly, either. Not with his hardening cock lying in Christian's hand.

Reluctant but determined, he shifted his hips and pushed Christian's hand away. He found his fingers couldn't let go of Christian's. Mind racing, Brandon lay there, legs hanging off the edge of the bed, pants unzipped, hard dick pushing up from under the waistband of his boxers, breath coming in shallow gulps as he tried to regain his perspective and some control over the situation.

God, he couldn't believe he hadn't heard Christian enter the room. He had to fight down the urge to react like an embarrassed adolescent, even if he did want Christian. He had to be in control of this. He couldn't afford to jump from one futureless relationship into another. He had to remind himself he'd only known Christian for a few days. He wasn't even Christian's type. There couldn't be a future with the handsome, adventurous archaeologist any more than there had been with Phil. He wished he could figure out what his type was. And where it hung out.

"We need to stop." Brandon turned his head slightly to avoid Christian's mouth as he tried to ignore him and reclaim his lips. He ended up breathing Christian's exhaled breath and the smell of lime and tequila reminded him of the kiss that had just ravaged him, leaving behind the taste of both ingredients. He wanted nothing more than to taste the flavors again, but he clamped his lips tightly together and shook his head, his gaze finally meeting Christian's imploring stare.

"Let me make love to you, Brandon." Pupils dark with passion, Christian murmured a noise in thwarted protest. His lips, dusky rose and full, brushed over Brandon's jaw and chin, searching teasingly for his mouth, asking permission with each soft caress. "Now. Here."

"I really can't. I'm -- I'm not available." Brandon couldn't keep eye contact with Christian when it came to discussing Phil. Now he felt even more like an embarrassed teenager. He scooted his upper body further out from under Christian, lamenting the loss of contact even as he did it.

"Where's Phil right now? What's he doing?" It was said gently, but it was still painful.

Christian rolled to one side, letting Brandon have more freedom to move if he wanted it. Neither one of them moved again for several tense seconds.

"That's not fair." Brandon turned his face away, voice low, the hurt evident even to his ears.

"No, it's *not* fair." Christian had a way of speaking that made whatever he said sympathetic and kind, even when it would have sounded condemning coming from anyone else.

"I meant your comment wasn't fair."

"I know what *you* meant." Undaunted by the accusation, Christian merely nodded and turned Brandon's face so they were eye to eye again. "*I* meant your situation."

The room rotated on its axis as Brandon sat up on the edge of the bed, tucking himself back under the elastic of his shorts. He couldn't have a serious conversation with his dick hanging out begging for attention.

"Listen, Christian. I like you." He licked his dry, swollen lips, tasted a hint of lime on them and heaved a sigh, eyelids sliding closed for a brief moment. "I like you a *lot.*"

When he looked back at a still silent Christian, a spark of unbridled passion settled in the man's marble gray eyes. Brandon's resolve started to crumble, the force of the expression coupled with the longing in his own heart.

He stood up to put some needed distance between them. "But I'm not someone who sleeps with every guy I'm attracted to." He shook his head and glanced away, ruefully zipping his jeans up. "Not when I'm seeing someone."

Christian smiled and stood up, moving in close to Brandon. "You're attracted to me?" he said, ignoring the other part of Brandon's statement.

Brandon snorted in disbelief. "Well, Christ, yes." He gestured at the man's tall, athletic physique, his wavy dark hair and broad shoulders, taking in his stunning eyes and brilliant smile all in one inclusive frenzied hand gesture. "Who wouldn't be?"

"There isn't anybody in my life, Brandon. Not for a long time now. " Hands gripped his arms above the elbows and Christian turned him until they were face to face. "I don't try to sleep with every guy I'm attracted to, either." The man's voice was soft and coaxing, sincerity and understanding packed into each word. "Just those I think I could fall in love with."

"What? Are you crazy?" Brandon could feel Christian's heated emotion all the way down to his toes. It started in his chest, rolled past his stomach, and then buzzed through his full, aching shaft and balls on the way to his feet. The force of Christian's words and intent made him short of breath. He couldn't tell if his heart was going to explode first, or his cock.

God, he wanted to believe this was real, but reason and past experience told him otherwise. He walked away, gaze drawn to the fading evening light casting long shadows on the walls. The noise from the small crowds of people out in the street magnified the nagging loneliness that had begun to push out the hurt and depression of Phil's desertion and betrayal. Brandon wanted to fill the gaping void in his life, even temporarily, but he knew he'd be in worse shape if he let his dick or his broken heart think for him right now.

"Let's be serious, Christian. I'm not even your type." It came out sounding like the lame excuse that it was. A silence followed that said more than all the words Brandon should have said. He stared out the window and tried to remember why he was in this exotic land, in a luxurious, sensual bedroom, talking his way out of having sex with a gorgeous, generous, and interesting man.

A light tread of footsteps on the thick carpeting preceded a presence hovering at his back. He could sense the body heat and tart scent of lime. Small puffs of air tickled the skin at his collar. A shiver made the five o'clock shadow on his jaw bristle in response. Sweat rolled down his back between his shoulder blades, only to be captured by his waistband.

A hand pressed at the small of his back and the moisture disappeared, either absorbed by the saturated cotton or evaporated by the heat of Christian's palm. His breathing became shallower and more rapid, waiting for Christian to break the silence.

"I think you're just my type."

The words were whispered in his ear so close that Brandon jerked in surprise. The warm breath on his neck raised a flash of gooseflesh. "That's because you're nuts."

A persistent tug on his shoulder made Brandon turn back around. "You, Detective Brandon King, are smart, quick-witted, inventive, and brave."

Christian's gaze was intense, bright, and hot like molten marble. It was amazing how much sincerity and trust he managed to pack into his expression. The pull to accept whatever he said tugged hard at Brandon's soul. He made it all believable.

A thumb rubbed over Brandon's parted lips, rough flesh on tender skin, the touch gentler than expected. If Phil touched his mouth, it was usually to clamp a hand over it to keep him quiet. "Plus, I think you look sexy as hell when you're breathless and all sweaty."

"Get real. I know what I look like." Brandon shrugged, resisting the urge to taste the thumb Christian held to the corner of his mouth, his hand cupping Brandon's jaw, fingers splayed across his cheek, holding him in place and comforting him at the same time.

"Do you?" Christian bent at the knees a little to keep eye contact when Brandon dropped his gaze. His hand gently forced Brandon's head up. The smile that met Brandon's gaze erased some of his embarrassment. "What do you see when you look in the mirror? Bet it's not the same thing everyone else sees."

"I see an ordinary guy no one is going to go out of their way to get to know. I see a guy who's more than a little bit afraid of being alone all of his life."

"Face it, Brandon, you're not afraid of losing Phil. You're just afraid. I listened to you when you told me about your dad leaving when your mom got cancer and how quickly she passed away. I understand you've been alone and lonely since she died. I know you don't want to end up alone to live out your life." Even though it was gently said, with tenderness and understanding, the words cut Brandon to the quick, revealing his innermost, never-voiced fears. "But guys like Phil are just using you and, honestly, you're using him."

"That's not true. I-I...l-love Phil."

"Phil's just the current means to fill your empty off-hours. I bet you're still lonely with him as your boyfriend."

Brandon flinched.

"I thought so." There wasn't any pleasure in his voice, only concern. "What's it going to be like when he expects you to still be his lover on the side after the wedding?"

"That isn't...I wouldn't...you don't know that."

Even Brandon didn't believe the protest. Phil *would* want to have his cake and eat it, too. And if Brandon's heart wasn't taken by someone else, Phil would get it, too. Part-time lover and full-time fool, that would be Brandon's next official title instead of "boyfriend."

"But you know it." Christian grabbed Brandon by the upper arms and forced him to look him in the eyes. "What you really need is someone who will love you with all their heart, love you back as much as you love them." He pulled an unresisting Brandon to his chest, his lips brushing Brandon's. "Someone like me."

Christian's words were sucked into Brandon's mouth and swallowed down into his chest to scorch a mark on Brandon's racing heart. He'd have answered if his lips hadn't been sealed to Christian's, his tongue dueling with the man's, then willingly submitting to having his mouth ravaged until he was gasping for air and his jaw ached from the force of the kiss.

His lips felt like they should be blistered and raw. His throat burned and his chest throbbed with a full, heavy feeling that left him giddy and confused. Maybe letting a new love come to him instead of working so hard to force the old one to remain *was* the better plan.

Suddenly, the trip became more of an adventure to Brandon than a quest to win back Phil's philandering heart. It was a journey to find his own heart. Maybe Phelan was right. Maybe he didn't want his old life back.

Allowing the pent-up anger to flare for the first time, Brandon pulled back slightly to meet Christian's stare. He hadn't realized just how much of his self-confidence the relationship with Phil had drained away from him. He was a cop, a detective, an officer of the law. True, he worked burglary now, where there were very few dangerous criminals to meet face to face, but he'd had his moments and he was trained to face dangerous times. He suddenly realized that these months of living in Phil's "closet" had done more damage to his self-esteem than had all the other failed, open relationships that had come before.

Maybe all this anxiety he was experiencing was his life opening back up again, and maybe, just maybe, he had a chance with someone like Christian.

He leaned forward and grabbed a rough, quick kiss from Christian's lips, his upper arms still held tight in Christian's grip, their bellies pressed together, their legs entangled, their bodies held upright by their sheer weight pressing against each other.

"Tell me why you're still alone, Christian. Why is someone who can have anyone still living alone?" The need to know the truth burned in Brandon's eyes. He could feel it radiating out of them, knowing the answer to this question would make or break this moment for them. Brandon knew he needed someone new in his life, but it had to be the right someone, not a new mistake.

Christian seemed to know it, too. "Because if, as you claim, I *can* have anyone, I can afford to wait for the *right* one."

He grabbed a handful of Brandon's hair with one hand and his ass with the other, pulling him in so close their straining dicks rubbed together. Christian ground his crotch against Brandon's, sending sparks of delight up Brandon's spine and a fresh wave of heat to the pit of his stomach.

Christian's teeth latched onto Brandon's lower lip and tugged at it, then let it slip away to firmly declare, "And that one appears to be you."

CHAPTER SIX

The kiss was long, rough, and blissfully ravenous. Brandon couldn't get enough of the taste of Christian's mouth. The faint hint of lime still lingered, mixed with a flavor so foreign and exotic he could only label it "passion." He thought he'd experienced passion before, but it hadn't felt this good, this raw.

He didn't think he had *ever* tasted it. Passion rolled over his tongue, seeped into his cells, and once there, multiplied. It spilled into his veins and flowed along, touching every part of his body -- muscle, bone, and flesh, a force so strong it created a static charge on his skin. He felt consumed, embraced by a dizzying sensation of pleasure and perfection. If he leapt from the shuttered window beside him, he knew he could fly.

Hunger rushed through him, moving hands and fingers, mouths and tongues, into a flurry of activity. Words lost meaning for Brandon, transformed into grunts and moans, primal groans of need and possession. He refused to question the passion winding its way through his soul, tying strings of want around his heart that swelled into tight, binding ropes.

The threads were rough and prickly, but the pain only served to heighten his desires, inflame the gorgeous ache in his groin that moved to explode in his chest. He suddenly realized he was experiencing love, evolving from lust and longing into real love at the very core of his being, all from a single kiss. It was nothing like the nervous tentative groping of his other first times with a new lover. This was bold, powerful, and empowering. It gave bliss a new meaning for Brandon. It was frightening and he never wanted it to stop.

They fumbled their clothing open and off with a newly found and unleashed fury fueled by a primal calling of man on man. The restrictive imperative to be gentle was discarded in the first bruising embrace and crush of lips to lips and cock to cock. This was hot, raw, and instinctive. No delicate flesh to worry about bruising when it occurred, and no mandate to woo with delicate touches and flowery words. Commitment and want were demonstrated in each spread palm rubbed over sizzling skin and every nip of teeth and thrust of tongue and hip. Brandon had never felt so overwhelmed, so connected, or so right as he did this moment.

Passion somersaulted in his lower abdomen and pounded under his ribs, his brain bombarded by a maelstrom of sensation and color. Naked, stripped to his bare essence in both the literal and figurative states, he wrenched his mouth away from Christian's before he lost the capacity, struggling to maintain some small measure of control.

He opened his eyes to meet Christian's dark, hungry stare. His gaze swallowed the image of the man's starkly handsome face made even more appealing by the desire and longing in his expression. Strong hands gripped Brandon tightly to Christian's chest, one wrapped around his back and the other kneading the taut muscles of his ass, groping, coarse fingertips exploring the rounded crease, teasing the hidden valley.

Brandon pushed back into the indelicate touch, begging for more, his hole clenched and waiting, his mind screaming for a caress, a slap, a jab of intensity to its puckered, anxious portal.

Christian grabbed his hair and pulled his head pulled back, mouth engulfed by Christian's, lips and tongue explored anew with a vengeance that sucked away his breath and sent a rush of excitement-filled blood directly to his swollen, straining cock.

Trapped between their sweat-sheened bodies, his dick slid freely, nudging hard at the base of Christian's shaft, burrowing into the nest of coarse hair, his own pre-cum chill against it. Brandon pressed down on Christian's shoulders, rising up to gain enough height to pair both iron-hard rods side by side. The heat increased and his pleasure soared, the flared cap of his cock catching on the bulging veins of Christian's shaft and the dip and curve of melding belly and hip.

He lost his attempt at setting up a grinding rhythm of thrust and rub when Christian's tongue entered his mouth at the same time a blunt, dry finger breached his entrance, both invasions abrupt, harsh, and delicious. The burn in his ass was thrilling, deep and welcome. No finesse was required; the thickness of stroking flesh over moist walls and fluttering muscles called to an animal urge deep in the recesses of his brain and he responded to it, grinding back to spear his ass on its invader. His hips twisted and bucked, each roll aimed at generating more friction between their shafts and more depth from the finger in his opening.

The rhythms of hot, slippery slide in front and hot, raw burn in his ass made Brandon groan, the guttural sound reduced to a whimpered moan muffled by Christian's thrusting tongue and roving lips that continued to devour him. He pulled back from the pressure of the kiss only to have the grip in his hair tighten enough to make his eyes water.

It felt good to be desired, to be denied the chance to back away because his lover's passion for him was too great to be casually released or discarded. This was true desire, true want, true love. Brandon could feel it in Christian's grip, see it in his passion-dark eyes, the black threads in the marble gray wider and more pronounced in the growing shadows of the falling sunset. This was something neither could walk away from when it was over. Brandon knew he couldn't, even if they never went any further than this. He was hooked. He prayed Christian was a man of his word.

Brandon's cock ached, his ass spasmed and fluttered, sparkling lights danced behind his eyelids while air rasped in and out of his deprived lungs. Blood pounded under his flesh, his pulse beating out a rapid rhythm he could feel at the base of his dick. His heart yearned for more, his body demanded more, and his instincts got him more.

Their frenzied dance of passion had moved them instinctively closer to the low, long bed, where graciously parted netting and open bedding awaited them. Cool sheets and plump pillows told stories of scorched flesh soothed by their touch and bodies angled and supported by their soft wedges. Brandon heard their tales in the humid, sex-scented air of the bedroom and knew he wanted to add their story of passion to the room's history.

Using a move he had used to take down uncooperative assailants, Brandon twisted and heaved, spun and tumbled, landing chest to chest atop Christian's solid, muscled frame, face to face, cock to cock. The kiss never broke; muscled, powerful arms linked wiry strong arms all the way from standing to falling. Now Brandon took control of the embrace, using gravity and his newly acquired freedom of movement to his advantage.

A silent chuckle from deep in Christian's chest vibrated through their chests and shimmied down Brandon's spine to his still rutting cock, each grunting thrust of his hips forcing a tight squeeze of his stretched rectal muscles. They gripped Christian's single, deeply embedded finger, then gasped open to protest the intrusion of a second digit.

The sensation of fullness in his ass expanded his dick. Brandon moaned into Christian's pliant, eager mouth, hips rocking, tongues playing, and ass spasming in a rhythm that was going to bring him off soon. It was too much too fast and he needed it to last. He pulled his mouth away from Christian's, barely managing enough clearance to allow his lips to form words.

"Wait. Wait, I don't want to come yet."

His breath came in short, labored puffs, his voice husky with passion, thick with urgency. His world turned upside down and what little breath had been in his lungs exploded out in a surprised grunt. His ass clenched, grinding down on the fingers wedged deep, a flash of discomfort jolted away by a brief, unexpected nudge against his prostate. The burn promised more and better things to come. Christian winked at him from above this time, a cocky grin on his reddened lips and a playfully dark look in his eyes.

"Let me see if I can help out with that." Christian stole a leisurely kiss before sliding down Brandon's body. He worked a few inches at time, licking patches of skin, nuzzling sensitive underarms and heaving ribs, teeth worrying swollen nipples and delicate belly button, on his slow and measured journey.

By the time Christian's knees hit the floor by the side of bed, Brandon's legs were sprawled wide in total abandon on either side of Christian's hips. While the new sensations were breathtaking and sensual, Brandon had regained control of his pending orgasm. Now his cock stood tall, curved slightly to one side, the slit glistening with beads of pearly white offerings captured in its deep groove, its bobbing crown eager for attention again.

Sheets balled into wrinkled handholds under his palms, Brandon's gaze was drawn to Christian's bold, smoldering stare. He watched as Christian trailed his tongue through the fine path of brown hairs that led from Brandon's navel to the base of his cock, then sighed, a minute tremble quaking his limbs, as the cool wetness traveled left, then right, scouring the sensitive creases between thigh and groin.

Eyes drifting closed in blissful delight, senses drowning in sensation and simmering waves of growing heat, Brandon jerked back to reality when his dick was swallowed down until the tip banged off the back of Christian's throat, spongy head slick over smooth palate and prodding tongue.

"Christ! Jesus, God, that feels good." Brandon squeezed his eyes shut, but the sheer intensity of Christian's soul pulled them open again. He saw the undisguised want in the gray eyes, felt it in the heavy hand gripping his wrist, recognized love and heartfelt desire and not just the fugitive lust, mediocre in substance and fleeting in depth like the look he'd often seen in Phil's expression.

Every tap of fingertip to prostate and bobbing suck on his cock acted like a salve to his wounded heart, mending it, soothing it, and making him whole again. Christian's caring and affection, his ability to know what turned Brandon on, where to touch and for how long only served to pull the ties forming between them tighter. Christian left Brandon speechless in a way no other lover ever had before. It was more than sexual need or urgency; it was almost mystical, frightening, and wonderful. Suddenly his whole world collapsed down to this moment in time, this room, this man. Nothing was important beyond these walls.

Brandon had a flash of insight and wondered if the totem's legend hadn't already influenced him. At this point he didn't care. This was real. This was happening. He and Christian were becoming lovers. They had a shot at a future together. Everything else was too far away in the future to worry about.

His cock jerked and his balls tightened. Threads of jarring ecstasy blazed along his nerve endings from the base of his dick to somewhere deep inside his chest. Its tendrils wound around his lungs and squeezed his heart, closed his throat, and then rocketed down to sizzle in the delicious burn in his ass. His asshole spasmed, clutching the firm, stiff fingers curled against his walls, rubbing a small seed of delight hidden there. Another slow press and the tip of a third digit spread his ring of muscle wider and Brandon came.

The orgasm exploded on him, no leisurely escalation like last time. It went supernova in a flash, hurtling Brandon into the vacuum of outer space. His lungs refused to work and even his cry of agonized triumph and total bliss went unheard, trapped in his closed throat, silent with the lack of air. Stars burst behind his eyelids and heat that rivaled the sun's scorching rays burned his body.

His back arched, his hips burrowed into the mattress, and a thrilling fullness rotated at his entrance between clenched cheeks. His hands left behind twisted folds of sheet, one to clamp onto Christian's still bobbing head to silently beg for mercy, and the other merely twisted over to latch onto the hand pinning it down.

Slowly, the room came back into focus. Christian licked his way back up Brandon's torso, from his now flaccid shaft to his heaving chest. He ended his explorations by lapping the sweat from Brandon's throat and sealing his lips to Brandon's, sharing the taste of their lovemaking mixed with his still burning desires.

"Fuck me."

The words were harsh, needy and low, more growl than request. They made Brandon's cock twitch and his nostrils flare, a spark of primal dominance forming in the pit of his abdomen. Christian wanted to be fucked. By him. It had been a long time since he'd had the pleasure of his cock nestled deep in the blistering heat of a lover. The thought revived his energy and his dick, the shaft once again plump and rising off his belly like a flower reaching for the sun.

As much as the idea appealed to him, safety and comfort appealed even more. "We'll need something. Lube, condoms... things."

"Got it covered, lover."

Christian crawled off the bed, dragging Brandon part of the way with him. On his knees again at the side of the bed, he extended one long arm and pulled his own travel pack to him from the spot at the end of the bed where Brandon had left it earlier. Seconds later he had Brandon sitting on the edge of the bed as he crouched between his legs.

Christian wrapped both his hands around Brandon's cock and balls, playing and stroking, bringing full hardness back to his shaft and making his sac heavy with need again.

His ass still ached, and for a moment Brandon almost offered it in place of Christian's, but the fiery passion in the other man's eyes told him this was something Christian needed right now. God knew Brandon was more than willing to enter a new relationship on a more even level than the ones he'd had with his past lovers. It had been a long time since he'd done anything but bottom, and it was an unexpected pleasure to be treated as an equal from the start.

He leaned down to kiss Christian as the man tore open a condom pack and deftly fitted it over Brandon's cock. His touch was sure and soothing, milking the shaft as it smoothed out the latex. A snap and a squeeze later, Brandon shivered as cool lube was slathered over the barrier, the gel warming with each palmed stroke.

When he was done, Christian tugged on Brandon's wrist to make him stand. Christian leaned forward over the edge of the low bed, chest resting on the mattress, ass in the air, knees on the Persian rug on the floor, legs wide to welcome Brandon between his thighs.

The air was thick with the smell of passion and sex, the sounds from the street muted and indistinct within the room. The temperature had dropped a few degrees with the setting sun, but the intensity in the room kept the heat high. Dust drifted in the few fading rays of light that filtered into the room between the slats of the shutters, and in the distance the bells of a temple rang out, the tone deep and startling like the sound of a kettle drum. Its notes reverberated through Brandon, electrifying him, spurring him to move and intensifying the surreal and highly erotic scene. This was so perfect he was almost afraid it was a dream, but the smell of lime and sex screamed "real" to his senses.

Brandon dropped to his knees behind Christian and wedged himself in close, sheathed cock rubbing the cleft of Christian's spread ass, his belly curved over it, his hands gripping the solid hips of his lover.

He bent over and kissed the valley of Christian's spine, lavishing as much attention on the man as Christian has given him. He raked his teeth over the wet skin, then soothed it with a lick and a kiss.

Christian arched back and pulled Brandon's head over his shoulder until their lips met. They lingered in a deep, thorough kiss as Brandon pressed forward, one hand guiding his dick to the puckered opening to Christian's body. The slick tip crushed against the ring of muscle, held motionless on the edge of expectation, then suddenly slid forward. Both men groaned, filling the humid air with soft grunts, hissed sighs, and whimpers of pleasure.

"So tight, so perfect." Sweat dripped off Brandon's chin to pool in the dip at the small of Christian's back. "God, you're amazing."

The firm ass melded against his groin swayed in a provocative swing that added a twist to Brandon's deep thrusts, magnifying the sensations that rippled along his shaft. Christian was hot, slick, tight, and so sexy Brandon wanted to fuck him, suck him, ride him and kiss him all at the same time. Christian reminded Brandon of a regal lion, his athletic body covered in rolls of flesh-toned steel, shoulders knotted with layers of sinewy muscle, broad chest molded to perfection, waist trim and tapered, ass round and firm, corded thighs and calves taut, all power and energy and primal magnetism.

Just thinking about Christian's physical presence coupled with his intelligence, wit, and straightforward personality pulled Brandon toward climax. Christ, he loved a man with a brain, a loving heart, *and* fabulous physical *ass*-sets.

He increased his thrusts, changing the angle of entry until Christian swore under his breath. He knew he'd hit the spot he was looking for when Christian began hammering his ass back against him, muscles clenched in a hot vise around his cock. He bent low and wrapped his arm under to take Christian's dick in hand, tugging fast and hard, grip tight, palm dry, and the friction high.

"Mine."

"Fuck, yeah!" Christian's groan was told to the sheets, but Brandon heard and pumped faster, the thrill of ownership being granted zipping through him.

The room was steeped in long, cooling shadows. The swirling ceiling fans snatched the shadows up and tossed them into the air, chilling the tiny rivers of sweat running down Brandon's back. His hips snapped a staccato rhythm, hammering his cock home, the slide and tug blissfully, unimaginably snug. His balls drew up, their wrinkled sac slapping hard against the base of Christian's, each jarring sway and hit of flesh to flesh sending a thrill of pending orgasm sharp and sweet directly to his plunging dick.

Suddenly the sight of Christian's hunched back, muscles rippling, unruly dark curls plastered on his tanned skin, and luscious mouth parted in rapture was too much for Brandon. Christian groaned low and long into the bed and the hard rod in Brandon's hand jerked and spit thin ropes of wetness down his hand. Brandon's own orgasm rumbled up from the base of his dick and rushed to erupt without any more announcement than a massive flash of fire that engulfed Brandon's entire body at once.

"Shit, Chris, I'm there."

Christian's deliciously begging ass held him captive. Each squeeze made Brandon imagine his heart was being drawn out through his cock and pulled straight into Christian's. He fell forward and pulled Christian's face to the side until he could kiss him, the image of their souls transferring from each other's body through kiss and cock playing out in his mind's eye, marking this instant on his soul. He felt completed and satisfied like he had never felt before.

Cock completely spent this time, Brandon eased out of Christian. He rested chest to back for a moment catching his breath, enjoying the fading buzz of climax, savoring the memory of Christian's body and touch. If for some reason this never happened again, he wanted to be sure he could relive it in his dreams.

Still panting, Brandon rolled off the condom, tied it and tossed it toward a corner, then crawled over Christian and onto the bed, hands wordlessly urging Christian to do the same. Once they got pillows under heads and bodies aligned, Brandon allowed exhaustion to rule. He collapsed on his back a foot from Christian's identical pose, letting the fans' breeze cool their skin while their recovering lungs regained their ability to breathe.

He glanced over at Christian, marveling at how quickly the other man had recovered from the physical workout. Christian gave him a beatific smile, which shone in his eyes as well as on his lips. Brandon couldn't help but return it.

Rising up on one elbow, Christian leaned over and kissed Brandon, the touch firm, decisive, possessive, thrilling. It was a claiming kiss, long and lavish, a kiss between lovers, one that said this was just the first time and there would be years of more to come. It was gentle, full of promises and demands. It seared Brandon's soul and bound his heart to Christian's.

He kissed back with like intensity, hoping to do the same to Christian's heart. He couldn't stand the thought that he might be in this on his own. As if reading Brandon's mind, Christian broke away, stared down into Brandon's anxious face and quietly said, "I love you."

"Love you." Barely able to mouth the words, Brandon blinked back sudden moisture and nodded.

Christian fell back on the bed and raised his arm. Brandon instinctively rolled under it, sliding up to Christian's side. He pillowed his head on the man's offered shoulder and wrapped his arm over Christian's chest as a heavy arm dropped on his back, strong fingers curved over his ribs.

Legs entwined, heart rate decelerating and mind reeling, Brandon wanted to talk, knew there was a lot to say, but exhaustion won the battle and he let sleep have its way with him. He felt bad right up until Christian's snore turned into the last thing he heard.

CHAPTER SEVEN

"Why did you insist on coming here? With me?"

Brandon smacked at something that stung his neck, wiping the flattened body away with a sheen of grimy sweat. The heat and humidity were nearly suffocating and it was still midmorning. They had been traveling for hours, forging a path through jungle growth, moving deeper into the wilds of the rain forest and away from all known human contact. He stared at the back of Christian's head and waited, catching a glimpse of his new lover's profile as they walked single file through the dense foliage.

If anything, Christian looked even sexier in his sweat-stained khaki shirt and matching explorer's pants, belt equipped with sheathed bowie knife and canteen slung over one shoulder to dangle at his hip. The canteen spent most of the time slapping the man's firm right ass cheek while he pushed his way through the jungle. Brandon knew this because he'd been staring at that ass since they headed out. He envied the canteen's comfortable perch.

Since last night, he envied anything that got to touch any part of Christian's tanned, firm, muscular body when he couldn't. The man's rippling, supple skin was addictive. He could still feel the sensation of the curly short hairs of Christian's chest and belly crinkling under his fingertips.

"Other than the chance to ogle your naked and very fine looking ass, Detective?"

The teasing was unexpected. He was so used to complying with Phil's demanding vows of silence, the playful, open remark took Brandon by surprise. Then a grin graced his lips and a rueful smirk brightened his dirt-streaked face. "Other than that, yes."

"That's easy." Christian cast a quick look over his shoulder at Brandon, but kept on forcing his way forward, following the tiny path the guide ahead of him cut, hacking away with a broad machete in his right hand, the swing and thrust showing the power in his muscular arms and back. "No archaeologist passes up a fully funded dig for a legendary artifact backed by the most mysterious and elusive collector in the field. It's a chance at fame and fortune. That alone will make the myth true. That's one of *my* heart's fondest desires – professional glory in my career circle."

"I might have believed that was all in the beginning--" Brandon's smile widened. He knew his grin looked a little lovestruck, but he didn't care. "--but now that I know you better, I'm not buying it. You're not that self-centered."

"Yeah?"

The pleased expression on Christian's face was worth the effort it had cost Brandon to be honest. Accepting what he knew to be less than the full truth from a lover just to keep the waters smooth hadn't worked out all that well in the past. He was determined not to walk that road again.

"Yeah. I'm a cop, remember? I can read people pretty well." An image of Phil, cocky and self-assured, flashed through his mind. A small frown furrowed his forehead, darkening his mood just a little. "Trust me, I know self-centered."

"Too much exposure lately?" The words were said in a gentle voice that took some of the sting out of them, but not enough to stop the color from rising in Brandon's cheeks.

"Maybe." Brandon shot Christian a sour look, but he couldn't deny the implication. "Even if I don't admit it, I know when it's there."

He hacked at the thick vegetation surrounding him, marveling at how it all seemed to grow back moments after they chopped it away. If he turned around, he could barely make out the path they'd cut out for more than a few feet directly behind them.

"What's the real reason you're here, Christian? I know there's more to it than the glory. And it's not my ass. We weren't sleeping together when you insisted on coming."

When Christian gave him a lecherous eyebrow wiggle, Brandon reconsidered his wording. "When you insisted on traveling with me around the world." That only got him a snorted laugh. "Get you mind out of the gutter, will ya?" Christian turned and reached back to covertly cup Brandon's thickening package. Brandon blushingly pushed his arm away and mock threatened him with the long knife in his hand. "At least until we finish this conversation. I want to know why you're here. For real." He glanced behind him at the trailing supply carriers, then hissed, "And leave both our asses out of it until later, okay?"

It felt good to be able to say that, to talk to and about a lover in the open. The local guide and three native carriers couldn't even hear him, but was it satisfying to say it out loud.

His heart missed a beat when Christian stopped cutting and turned to study him for a full minute, silently appraising him, eyes full of something Brandon couldn't put a name to just yet.

"I suppose you have a right to know. Now that we're more than just two strangers on a wild quest." He must have seen the panic that blossomed in Brandon's expression because Christian smiled and shook his head, sending beads of sweat off his chin into the surrounding leaves. "Nothing ominous, lover. Just long. I'll bend your ear when we break for camp, okay?"

"It's okay if you say it's okay. I trust you."

Christian winked and moved deeper into the undergrowth.

Brandon returned to pushing and hacking away jungle growth, the flutter in his chest more from the reaction to Christian's wink and use of the term "lover" than from a continued sense of dread. Something undefinable in Christian's eyes told him it would be all right.

A bird flew into a bush nearby, its fluffy gray body landing like a tiny cloud on the branch, its voice adding a colorful squawk to the droning insect buzz and the rustle of the treetops alive with unseen life. Brandon wondered at the odd brush of white on one side of its ebony beak that ran up into its head feathers as if the bird had bumped against a freshly painted white fence. It made the bird stick in his mind and gave him something else to concentrate on besides the heat and the exhaustion of the march.

The trek grew harder the closer they came to the destination listed as the last rumored location of the temple they were searching for -- the lost temple of Karrtikeya. The temple was the anointed home of the statue of the Hindu god reputed to have been a warrior who loved only battle. So much so that he'd had no use for women. Brandon thought it was somehow fitting two gay men should go in search of Karttikeya's statue.

He snickered at the thought that maybe Phelan had hoped his gaydar would help him find Karttikeya and win him the prize others hadn't been able to accomplish over the years. Christian told him the lost temple had been focus of at least six other expeditions over the last hundred years. All but one had located the temple, but none had been successful in finding the statue. Two of the smaller expeditions, two-man parties like theirs, were never heard from again.

Their present guide had even been a part of the last attempt sixteen years ago. He couldn't explain exactly what had happened to the missing men, but he was firmly convinced that the powerful, ancient temple guardian has been displeased with the explorers. He said the men had left the campsite to explore the temple gates on their own one evening just before nightfall, thinking the setting sun would give them a new perspective on the temple, and never returned. No trace of them could be found the next morning. It was as if they had never existed.

Brandon wanted to chalk the farfetched story up to poor communication between them and the locals, but their guide spoke English and Christian knew enough of the local dialect to get his point across to the local men.

Dressed in the traditional lungi, a sarong wrapped around the waist with a single knot worn tucked up to work in, the men acted as beasts of burden, carrying all the needed supplies and water with them. Christian had insisted they travel light, bringing only a small tent with netting to keep out the worst of the biting bugs at night, light cots to keep them off the snake- and spider-infested ground, and the usual compact freeze-dried food rations and water.

The extra carriers had been hard to find and even harder to persuade to accompany them into this part of the jungle. Days into the rain forest, all three supply men were becoming jumpy and slow, constantly muttering among themselves. The guide, Hari, yelled and threatened them with the loss of the four dollar a day pay, a rate ten times the standard daily pay for a workday in this region, and they stayed, but they weren't happy about it. Always one to pick up on emotions, their unease made Brandon jumpy as well.

Right now Hari was in the lead, slashing out a meager path that he and Christian widened as they followed the rail-thin but surprisingly strong man. The nervous carriers were trailing behind three yards further away than they had been two hours ago. Brandon was sure they'd be missing entirely by nightfall.

◊ ◊ ◊ ◊ ◊

"A jungle babbler. I wonder how it got here."

"What?" Brandon looked into the forest, following Christian's gaze. It was difficult to make out anything but tones of green on green, but a flash of white finally caught his attention. He turned sideways on his campstool to get a better look.

"That bird." Christian gestured off into the brush, using two fingers to point as Brandon was quickly noting the other man always did. It was such a simple thing, but it was unique and made the small gesture more powerful. A lot of Christian's mannerisms were strong and unusual.

Christian had told Brandon some about his past, growing up all over the world, traveling with an adventurous aunt and uncle who had raised him after his mother died. Raised to be highly independent and self-confident, he had caught the bug for exploration and travel at an early age. Brandon had already discerned that his knowledge on so many unique things was as vast as it was random.

"It's a jungle babbler."

A plump gray bird teetered on a branch heavy with limp vines choking it. The downy bird looked out of place in a tropical jungle, but it blithely squawked out its own trademark tune.

"That one? The gray bird?" Sitting still was becoming difficult. Standing, Brandon chewed on the last of his lunchtime ration of dried fruit and meat, washing each swallow down with a sip of tepid water, barely resisting the urge to gulp the liquid and pour half the canteen over his grimy face and neck.

He liked heat, but this amount of humidity made it difficult for him to adjust. Without his usual candies and large quantities of strong coffee, he found himself constantly nauseous and irritable. He'd have paid big money for a straight sugar rush and a tall, iced espresso. "I think it likes us. It's been following us all day."

"How can you tell it's the same bird?" The expression on Christian's face was plain curiosity. His voice wasn't disbelieving, only tinged with a surprising edge of anxiety.

"The white streak on its beak and head. It looks like someone splashed paint on it. That can't be natural, a color streak on its beak into its feathers."

"No, it's not." Brandon could hear confusion in Christian's voice as the man joined him to watch the bird. "What's more unnatural is it even being here. Jungle babblers don't live in this region of India. This is too far north for them. Way too far. And they don't migrate."

The bird's off-key voice and sharp tone contrasted with the diminishing din of insects and the occasional howl of something unfamiliar. The howl had become more frequent the higher up the mountainside they climbed. It was unnerving to Brandon. The howl sometimes seemed angry and other times almost like a plea to his untrained ear. Christian explained it away as a harmless monkey, but even he looked puzzled when it dogged their trail all day long.

All three of the carriers were watching the bird now, muttering to each other. Hari barked a tense command at one of them when he fell to his knees and began to pray, a fast frenzy of garbled speech and mournful grunts even Brandon could understand were pleas of some type. The man rose to his feet, but the praying continued, low and desperate.

"Then what's it doing here?" Brandon frowned, his gaze drawn back and forth between the bird and the men. "What's wrong?" He jerked his head at the huddled group of carriers, picking up on their nervous energy, but unable to comprehend why the mere sighting of a small bird was creating such a reaction.

"They think this is a bad omen. The bird doesn't belong here." Christian glanced at the men with a frown that mirrored

Brandon's, marring his handsome, tanned brow. "This mountainous region isn't suited to them. It's all thickly wooded hills, plateaus, deep valleys, waterfalls, rivers, marshes, and streams here. They prefer the drier climate and vegetation to the south. We're in a part of the Himalayan range now. I'm really surprised it's survived. It has a dozen predators here."

"Looks pretty healthy to me. It's been keeping up with us. I've seen it in the trees all morning." Brandon stepped closer to the babbler's perch. The bird called out and moved a few inches toward him, its sharp squawk making the carriers chatter among themselves.

"Hm. Weird."

Without looking back at Christian, Brandon called out over his shoulder, "That's your professional opinion, O Great White Explorer Carter? *Weird*? Ha! I could have said that."

Staring at the tiny bird, Brandon imagined it stared back at him. Its loud, two-syllable squawk became less shrill, its song a bit more tuneful to Brandon's ear. The rise and fall of noise almost sounded like his name. He shook his head, but the tune didn't change from a singsong cry of *Bran-don*.

He pulled open his canteen and gulped down two large mouthfuls of water. The heat of the jungle was getting to him. Birds were talking to him now. Lord, he needed some coffee. With sugar. He turned away from the bird, but found watching Christian's behavior just as unnerving.

"No. I don't think you're getting it, Detective. The weird part is there aren't any other birds in the tree. Anywhere." Christian slowly rotated on his heel, gaze scanning the hillside and vegetation. "Look around, Brandon; the trees, bushes, they're all empty. There should be at least a dozen different species flying around. There were this morning when we broke camp."

A howl that was closer to a blood-curdling screech cut the air. Christian's frown furrowed deeper and the carriers became silent. Brandon stepped back, his shoulder making contact with Christian's as they moved in a circle, back to back, studying the trees. The air was oddly still, except for the occasional, random repeated screech that reminded Brandon of a cat in pain.

The temperature was over one hundred degrees, but a shiver skittered down Brandon's spine as sweat rolled down his temples.

Hari moved from the perimeter of the makeshift campsite to stand nearer to Christian. He scanned the entire area repeatedly, dark eyes nearly black, mouth furiously working over an old wad of tobacco chew. He spit a stream of brown into the undergrowth, lips pulling back to reveal a row of crooked yellow teeth. Dressed in the same traditional lungi as the carriers, his gnarled hands worried the waist knot of the sash, belying his terse reassurances to the frightened men.

The babbler leapt from its branch and landed on a broad leaf that looked too flimsy to hold its weight, but the leaf didn't even quiver under the bird's feet. The new spot brought it to eye level with Brandon. The *Bran-don* cry split the air, magnifying the unnatural hush. The call was clear and crisp, enunciated so well that this time even Christian frowned and muttered, "What the hell?"

Unwilling to pull his gaze away from the fascinating creature, Brandon lowered his voice so the men couldn't hear him. For some bizarre reason, he hoped the bird couldn't, either. "That was my name, wasn't it? That's not normal."

"Nope." It was a short snap of a response, tension evident in Christian's defensive body language. "Not even a little." Discarded machete reclaimed and hefted in one hand, his obvious apprehension kicked Brandon's up a notch.

"Should have known." Another earsplitting screech echoed off the tropical canopy, much closer this time. "Nothing about this trip has been anywhere near the 'normal' scale."

Despite the foreboding atmosphere, or maybe because of it, Brandon felt a thrill of sexual excitement glow warm and heavy between his legs. His cock swelled and his balls tightened, drawing up to his body.

The men turned as one, gazes darting between the still calling babbler and the darkening jungle, searching for the source of the cry. Not a leaf moved; not an insect buzzed. It was as still as a graveyard until the muttered prayers started up again off to one side.

"I'll take that as a compliment." Attention still focused on the bird, Christian took a moment to flash Brandon an exaggerated, rakish leer over his shoulder. They broke away and stood side by side, thighs and arms touching, fingers brushing.

"Ego as big as your..." Brandon left the rest unsaid, gesturing vaguely at Christian's groin, gaze eyeing the respectable bulge in the front of the other man's pants. Apparently danger was an aphrodisiac for both of them. He couldn't help the twisted smile that tugged at his lips.

"Big ego, then." Grinning, Christian winked seductively. "Guess I'll have to see if I can't keep it under better control."

"Don't even think about it, hotshot." His voice shook a little from lack of caffeine and sugar, but it was strong and determined. "I staked my claim on that particular real estate last night. I kind of liked it out of control, thank you."

"I'll remember that. No control, got ya, lover."

They hadn't heard anything advancing toward them, but suddenly a section of the jungle came alive. The foliage shimmered and the ground under their feet shuddered, with one long, heart-stopping, unidentified howl accompanying the violent trembling.

"Something's coming, Chris. Be ready."

Both men crouched low and dropped into a fighting stance. Christian replaced his machete with a rifle that Hari had grabbed from a frantic, retreating carrier and handed to him. Brandon's practiced hand automatically claimed the nine-millimeter handgun nestled on his hip with which their resourceful guide had mysteriously presented him shortly after losing sight of the tiny village. Brandon didn't question where it had come from. He was just grateful to have it now. The worst part about leaving the US had been leaving his service piece behind.

The howl rose to an inhuman pitch that rivaled the best Hollywood horror flick's heroine's cries, held the high note, then abruptly stopped, leaving an eerie void in its wake. Slowly the insect buzzing began to drone and the fluttering of birds could be heard in the treetops. Brandon spun around to face the babbler, only to find it missing from its branch. There wasn't a sign of it anywhere.

The incoherent prayers disappeared as well. Brandon turned to the huddle of men to see why, only to find that they had vanished along with the frenzied chants. The underbrush where they last stood didn't give a single clue as to where they had run. The thick green brush, tall grasses, and broad leaves were calm, thick, and seemingly undisturbed. No one remained with Christian and Brandon except a wide-eyed Hari.

CHAPTER EIGHT

"So what do you think happened out there today? Where did the carriers go?" Brandon dropped onto the narrow canvas cot butted up beside the length of Christian's cot, mosquito netting completely encircling them. "I heard them muttering something about a 'mandy bug gun'? What's that?"

"*Mande Burung.* Jungle man."

"Tarzan? They were frightened of Tarzan?"

"No. It's the Indian version of the Abominable Snowman, Bigfoot, a terrifying monster. They think he's the guardian of the Temple of Karttikeya. It's the local myth."

"Whatever was out there this morning wasn't a myth. Myths don't make the ground shudder."

"You're right. And they don't leave behind broken pottery." Christian pulled out the colorful shard of pottery which he had found on the ground earlier while he and Brandon were clearing away more of the vegetation from around the campsite. "These are fresh breaks. The clay is still porous and the edges aren't packed with soil. It's got to be a hundred years old, but it's only been broken and left behind in the last twenty-four hours."

To Brandon, it had just been a piece of broken plate or cup, but it obviously meant more to Christian. The archaeologist had reverently brushed it off, carefully wrapped it in his only handkerchief and slipped it into a side pocket for safekeeping. Now he was examining the symbols and foreign lettering on the chunk of useless ceramic.

Head pounding, Brandon rubbed a hand over his gritty neck and then up to his sweat-sheened temple. Even the soothing massage didn't help. He needed coffee, a simple cup of coffee, about twenty ounces tall, and all would be right with the world. They could even serve it in a broken mug made out of the same stuff as Christian's new treasure as long as they put coffee in it.

"Problems?"

"Headache. I miss my Sparkles and my coffee." Brandon listlessly dropped his arm to his chest and rolled his eyes, critically studying the surrounding dense vegetation. The squawking of the jungle birds had recently been joined by the screeching and chatter of a troop of monkeys. Brandon hadn't seen them yet, but he could hear them. The endless noise pounded in time with his pulsing headache. "Why hasn't anybody put a Java Café out here yet?"

"I don't think that particular chain extends outside the States yet." Christian snorted and leaned down to gently run a hand over Brandon's forehead. His hand was cool compared to Brandon's skin, and it dulled the pain for a moment.

"I can't do anything about the candy addiction, but as far as the caffeine goes, try one of these." Christian dug around in his battered backpack, eventually pulling out a small white box with the logo of a local pharmacy back in the States. He tossed it in the air and Brandon automatically caught it.

"What's this?"

"Chewable caffeine. It should help ease some of your worst symptoms."

Brandon gave Christian a "how did you know I'd need this?" frown.

Christian chuckled. "By the time we'd spent one day together, I suspected you might have a little problem on the trip." Awe and disapproval mixed in his tone. "You must drink two gallons of coffee a day, Brandon. Your kidneys are probably ten years older than you are, by the way you make them work. *And* when we get back, I'm buying stock in the company that makes those candies you're always eating. My retirement will be set."

"Yeah, well, we all have our vices." Fingering the gum pack, Brandon jutted his chin out to indicate the shard in Christian's hand. "Yours is collecting useless, broken..." He waved a hand through the air, vaguely searching for the right term and failing. "...things."

"They may be broken, but they aren't useless. I still see the beauty and value in them. Their history is what makes them special." Suddenly Brandon wasn't sure Christian was talking about the shard any more. The intensity in Christian's eyes and voice was too intimate, too direct. He felt the man could see straight into his scarred soul. "They're priceless, even if a bit battered by time. Broken *things* can be mended with patience and a little determination."

"Yeah?" Brandon stuck a piece of gum in his mouth and chewed.

"Yeah. And I'm a determined, patient man." Real affection and caring shone in Christian's eyes, enough to make Brandon's eyes water and his throat tighten.

"That's good to know." He swallowed past the tightness in his throat and returned Christian's gaze. "In case I haven't said this, I'm glad you came with me." Brandon rubbed both of his eyes, trying to wipe away the remaining burn from the sudden tears and the sweat that had run into them all day. "But I still want to know why you came. Really."

His headache waned a bit and Brandon popped another gum square into his mouth. The burn and rush of exploding caffeine being sucked into his system was euphoric.

"Take it easy on that stuff. You're only supposed to chew one at a time." He tried to grab the gum back, but Brandon moved it out of his reach. "Fine, stay up all night. You can take the next watch after Hari."

"No problem. Now, you were saying?"

Christian settled back on his own cot. "It's easy. Like I said before, I want to meet the Collector. He's a mystery man. Lots of knowledge and power in this business of archaeology. He knows just about everyone and everyone wants to know him, too. I want to know him."

"That's it? A need to network? You came all this way, following a lead that's based completely on an ancient, fantastic, centuries-old myth and crazy local superstitions?" Anger made Brandon's voice louder and his words curt. Distrust made them quiver. "Why am I not getting a warm feeling about this?"

The silence was more of an answer than Brandon wanted. He liked to talk things out, not sidestep them or tolerate them in silence. He stared hard at Christian and forced the next words reluctantly past his lips. "Are you using me? Not just to get to the statue, and get to the Collector, but me? 'Cause I have to know that right now."

The silence dragged on even though Christian's eyes begged him for understanding.

This was like a blow to the abdomen. Brandon was light-headed. He found it difficult to breathe. Jesus, why did he always pick this type? Was there an invisible sign on his forehead that said "use me"?

"Okay, come first light, we hit the trail, find the temple, bag the statue and head home." He yanked his cot away from Christian's and pulled it as far away as possible while still keeping it under the netting. He was pissed, but he wasn't stupid. Rumors had it that the insects in this region of the forest hills could drain a person dry in a single night. There had been actual cases of it. At least, they had said it was the insects.

Brandon threw himself onto his side, back facing Christian, eyes wide open and staring out into the rapidly falling night.

"There's more." It had taken several minutes, but the opening had finally come.

As hard as it was, between the burst of gum-induced caffeinated energy and the anxiety of their first fight, Brandon lay still and waited. He wanted to hear what Christian would say, but he was exhausted and his head was proving to be a major distraction. The gum only helped a little. He was pretty sure he'd have to chew the whole box at once to get close to the levels he was used to.

"This has nothing to do with 'us'. That hasn't changed. I still feel the same about you. This has to do with me, my past."

Turning over so he could watch Christian's expression and look into his eyes while he talked, Brandon tucked an arm under his aching head and studied his lover's face. Christian looked drawn, thoughtful, and a little embarrassed.

"I told you I was raised by my aunt and uncle after my mother died." He waited until Brandon nodded. "What I didn't tell you was that my father was responsible for her death. At least, he believed he was and I agreed with him -- until a few years ago."

Curiosity was numbing the anger. If there was one thing he understood, it was the pain of complex family dynamics. Growing up gay with a hard, stoic father who bailed the moment his mother was diagnosed with cancer, he often felt like the poster boy for a dysfunctional family.

"What happened to make you change your mind?"

"I became an archaeologist, just like him. When I was born, he was in the field. On a project too important to ignore in a land too far away and isolated to easily leave. He knew my mother was in the best medical hands and that she had her sister and her husband for support. What he didn't count on was my mother's delicate mental state and how hard postpartum depression would affect her. To make a long story short, she killed herself when I was a barely a month old. Overdosed on her antidepression meds and a few other drugs. He was deep in a Brazilian rain forest and never even found out about her death until months later. I was living with my aunt and uncle. They tell me he came to see me once when he signed over guardianship of me to my aunt. He's never set eyes on me again to this day."

"I'm sorry, Chris. That's terrible."

"That's what I thought for most of my life. But once I became an archaeologist myself and went on my first dig, I understood his passion and dedication." Those same emotions poured into Christian's voice and animated his body language. Brandon could see the excitement and enthusiasm radiate from the man.

"I suddenly knew why he was gone all that time. How his work could become the center of everything, blocking out the rest of the world. It transports you to places and times that aren't your own. You relive history through each new piece of broken pottery." He palmed his own discovered fragment of the past, his touch slow and gentle despite his fevered speech. "You can literally see the lives of these people, entire cultures that have been lost and forgotten, in each new wall drawing or painted artifact. I understand now how he could shrug off the technological comforts and safety of the world he left at home as a low priority. The real danger and mystery was what he was facing; his work, his explorations would seem so much more important. He didn't expect an attack from the home front."

His eyes shone with the wonders of what he was describing, but Brandon could see the hurt in them as well. "So tell him. You find the remains of long lost civilizations, certainly you can find one man, especially one I'm guessing is well-known in your field."

"He is -- was, yes. But he dropped out of circulation a number of years back. I've received word of him every now and then, but I can't find him or any of his friends who'd actually laid eyes on him in years."

"How do you know he's still alive, Chris? Maybe all of this is for nothing."

"The same anonymous source that contacts me about once a year. A letter arrives each year around my birthday. Just a short note updating me on his health, which is suffering the effects of age, old wounds, and past illnesses contracted from over decades in the field, and letting me know he's aware of my accomplishments. No matter where I am, at that time of year, the letter always finds me. It's uncanny. He always knows where I am and how to reach me."

"That says money and power, Chris, not the work of a reclusive old man." Brandon's training kicked in and he stopped himself from pointing out the flaws in Christian's reasoning. The pain in Christian's voice when he talked about his father made his chest ache almost as much as his head. He wished he felt as much for his own dad. He'd spent a lifetime around the distant man and still didn't care about him half as much as Christian did for his father. "Are you sure the information is real?"

"That's why I need to meet the Collector. My father's got to have the help of someone like this man to do that. The Collector *must* know my father. He'll know how to reach him. He can help me find him before it's too late. That's *my* greatest desire."

"You don't need the statue for that." Brandon sat up on the edge of the cot. He wanted to hold on to Christian and tell him it would all work out, but he wasn't sure of that himself. "I can take you with me when I return the statue."

"But he could always refuse. You said yourself, you didn't actually meet him, only his assistant." Christian was beginning to sound desperate and very determined. "The statue would guarantee the Collector would help me. He wouldn't have a choice then."

Brandon studied the burning need in Christian's eyes, saw the tension and strain in his body language and the way his fists clenched, and he knew they weren't going to solve this. No matter how great a guy Christian was, how wonderful a lover he was, how caring he could be, once again Brandon was involved with a man who put his own needs above everything else. This was Brandon's quest for happiness. Christian was supposed to be along to help *him*.

"I didn't come all this way to risk everything, including my life, to fail, Chris. I need that statue. True, Phil isn't my heart's desire any more. You are. The question here now is, if we find the statue and the legend is true, do we both benefit from it? Or is one of us going home empty handed?" Anger was starting to build again.

"I don't think we have to compete for this, Brandon. If I'm truly your heart's desire, you don't need the statue. I'm already yours." The passion and need still burned in Christian's eyes, but Brandon wasn't sure if it was for him or for the statue, or hopefully, for both. "But I'd still need it to find my father."

Insecurities flared and past mistakes flew up in Brandon's memory like ashes in a bitter wind. He needed time to think and his head hurt too much to figure it all out right now. "I'm just not sure, Chris. This is all happening too fast. I'm ... just not sure." Brandon gave a helpless shrug and shook his head. "About anything."

Angry at the infamous Collector, the prim Ms. Phelan, Christian, and the entire universe for dealing him one more convoluted, impossible relationship, Brandon threw himself down on the cot. Giving Christian a challenging glare, he stuffed two more pieces of caffeinated gum into his mouth, ignoring the sharp burn and bitter taste. Heart heavy and head aching from the worst headache he'd had in ages, he tossed the gum box down beside him on the cot and lay down, arms crossed over his chest and a frown on his face. He shot Christian another glare. The patient, silent look on the man's face only made Brandon feel worse and he lashed out, feeling totally as adolescent as he sounded.

"I take that back. There is one thing I'm sure about. I don't care if the whole damn jungle comes down on us, I want a fire in the morning and I want coffee. A whole pot of hot, delicious, strong-enough-to-strip-flesh-off-the-bone coffee!" He flipped onto his side, facing away from Christian.

The screeching monkeys and heat from Christian's stare boring into his back made it harder than normal to fall asleep, but the small bursts of caffeine were a comfort to his system and eventually Brandon faded off. His last conscious thought was to wonder if the huge yellow eyes he saw in the vegetation staring back at him were his imagination or just a guilty conscience conjuring demons to plague him in his sleep.

CHAPTER NINE

His back ached and his head throbbed, but the few hours of sleep Brandon had managed to grab before and after taking his turn at guarding the campsite had helped clear his mind. Once he realized he was angry at the situation they had been thrust into and not Christian, his attitude mellowed.

If Christian was serious about them, statue or no statue, he really didn't need it. He'd decided days ago this trip was more of an adventure for him, a distraction from all the problems he'd left behind, than a quest for some ridiculous mystical power that could grant "happily ever afters." Real life wasn't cured with magic. And being with Christian felt real and it felt right. He'd have to learn to trust a whole lot more again if he ever wanted to find his own "happily ever after."

By the time he'd chugged down the last drop of the pot of coffee Hari had made, he was feeling sheepish about his behavior the night before. The long, lonely night had been made even worse by the repeated appearance of the staring yellow eyes in the nearby vegetation. He knew they weren't real. No one else had mentioned seeing them. The eyes couldn't just be visible to him if they were real. They would stare at him from a few feet away but when he turned his head, they would be in the undergrowth on the other side of the clearing almost immediately. Most of the time they weren't there at all. He blamed it on his dulled but persistent headache, his overtaxed nerves, and his guilty conscience.

"Feeling better?"

"Yeah. Much, thanks."

Sighing in satisfaction as he lowered his empty tin cup, Brandon nodded and knelt down beside Christian to help him douse the fire. Christian had been charitable enough to not to say anything past "good morning" until Brandon had managed to down at least half the pot. By the time he was savoring the last bitter cup, he and Christian were back on cordial speaking terms.

"You check with Hari to see where we're headed off to today and I'll finish up here, okay? That way we can get on the road faster." Brandon glanced around at the seemingly impenetrable forest surrounding them. "If there was a road."

Christian smiled and reached out to brush something off Brandon's upper lip with his thumb. The touch was gentle, intimate, and assuring. "No filter in the drip chamber. You've got coffee grounds on you." He brushed over the other side of Brandon's parted mouth, the move slower and more seductive. "Maybe I should just wash them off."

"Let me help you with that." Heated gazes locked together, Brandon turned his head far enough to capture Christian's thumb with his mouth. He sucked the digit in and rolled his tongue over and around it, thoroughly wetting it with each lick and caress of his tongue. Slowly easing his head back, he let the thumb pop out of his mouth, then nuzzled it as Christian rubbed the slick pad over his lips.

Just when the tension reached the strip and let's fuck stage, Christian drew his hand away with a smile that promised to finish what they'd started soon.

"Later, lover," said Brandon.

Christian stood up and dusted ashes and dirt off his hands. "Deal." He looked skyward, a frown furrowing his forehead. "It looks like it might rain soon. The quicker we're underway, the better. Hari said we were close last night and I'd rather be in a temple than outside when the rain hits. It can be torrential at times." He moved off to where Hari was busily distributing the remaining supplies among their backpacks.

Using his empty cup for a shovel, Brandon scooped dirt into the fire until it smoldered and spit smoke and ash. He stirred it with the end of a discarded stick and poured the grounds from the cooling coffee pot on top. A low rumble caught his attention and he glanced up through the billowing gray smoke from the extinguished flames. What looked like a huge shadow blotted out several square feet of the thick forest ten feet away.

There were plenty of shadows in this jungle and this one wasn't that much different than most until it moved. It moved, it rumbled again, and it had a pair of huge yellow eyes that stared back at Brandon. The most disconcerting part to the detective was that the eyes were almost as tall as he was while on his knees. Whatever it was, it was very big.

Brandon froze in place, eyes locked with the creature's unwavering glare. Voice soft, almost casual, as if the beast would know from his tone he was preparing to defend the camp, he called out to the others. "Chris? Do you have a rifle handy?"

"Yeah. Why?" Christian's answer was light and playful, responding to Brandon's tone. "I hate to be the one to break it to you, but I don't think you can kill a fire with one, Detective."

Still crouched low on one knee to stir the dying fire, Brandon slowly rolled a still-glowing log out of the ashes into a clump of grass. A wisp of smoke rose from the dry blades, burning his eyes and giving him a slim thread of hope. He wished he and Christian hadn't been so meticulous about making the campsite fireproof. He could have done with a wall of burning grass between him and whatever was facing him. He slowly straightened his spine, gaze never breaking away from the unblinking yellow stare.

"Think I can kill a *mande burung* with it?" He heard his voice shake and hoped Christian would hear it, too. "I don't think my handgun is going to make much of an impact here."

"Brandon?" His name was called softly, followed by the slide and click of the rifle being primed and readied. His own hand slipped down to pull the gun at his side out of its holster. Even useless, it gave him the illusion of power and protection. Right now he could use that reassurance. Jungle beasts were a whole different ballgame than street punks and burglars. The rifle sound sent a stab of relief through him that was short-lived, as the creature reacted to it as well.

Its clawed paws seemed to almost reach Brandon before the creature's head and body even emerged from the forest. With a deafening roar, the shadow grew taller and broader as it exploded out of the shuddering foliage, teeth bared, massive jaws open wider than the circumference of Brandon's head.

He instinctively ducked and rolled, trying to get nearer the small blaze that had finally started in the grass. On his back, he aimed for a belly shot directly into the beast and fired, uncertain of his target when faced with an unbroken sheet of sable fur and muscle. He fired off three shots before the animal passed over him, sure each one hit something in the beast.

Two rifle shots echoed in the clearing. Brandon rolled to a kneeling position, gun ready. He narrowed his focus to the only threat in the area and pumped his gun's remaining bullets into the clear target of the charging beast's back. It stood on its hind legs, dwarfing Christian, who stood to its left, and towering over Hari, who took a harsh blow from one mighty paw and crumbled under the animal's weight as it went down.

A few scant seconds after it had begun, the attack was over, the dark animal still and unmoving, lying on one side in the dirt, the guide's maimed and lifeless body several feet away where it had been tossed by a final sweep of a clawed paw.

Brandon blinked away the bugs that buzzed around his face and rose to his feet, gun still trained on the creature. He stamped out the small blaze on the ground, eyes darting from Christian to the animal to what was left of their guide and back to the downed marauder. He holstered his empty weapon and slowly advanced, picking up Hari's dropped rifle on the way to Christian's side.

"You all right?" He quickly scanned Christian for injuries, dismissing the bloodstains on his clothing and arms as splatter from the dead guide. Their gazes met for a moment and he could see the immense relief in Christian's face. He was a shade paler than his tan should have let him look.

"I think you did just fine with your handgun, Detective King." His voice was as relieved as his expression, a breathy quiver barely heard in the last two words. "That was some fancy outmaneuvering there."

Without waiting for a comeback, Christian grabbed Brandon around the neck and roughly pulled Brandon close. He buried his face in Brandon's dark curls to whisper, "I thought I'd lost you." He pressed a long, hard kiss to Brandon's temple. "Christ, I just found you and I thought I'd already lost you."

Brandon ran his free hand over Christian's chest, firmly patting the hard-muscled pecs, his hand fisting Christian's shirt, tugging strongly enough to shake the taller man, a mindless physical gesture that reassured and comforted them both. It was a long moment before either released his grip.

Hefting his rifle, Brandon used it to point at the creature and gave his lover a questioning lift of one eyebrow. After a nod from Christian, they both slowly approached it, weapons ready. The creature hadn't moved since it fell and its chest wall or abdomen hadn't moved in the effort to take a breath in several minutes. Its yellow eyes were half-open in death and its long tongue lolled out between parted jaws. Crouching down by its massive chest, Christian relaxed enough to really look at it thoroughly.

Instincts screaming caution, Brandon joined him, down on one knee and rifle still aimed at the beast. "What is it? It looks like a lion, but I've never seen one this dark before."

"And you won't see it again. This one shouldn't even be here. It's an Asian lion. You can tell by the big black tufts at his elbows, longer tufts on his tail, and the smaller mane. Black patches at the back of the ears and that skin fold at his belly mark him as a Persian."

"Persian? Didn't I hear somewhere those are extinct?"

"There are only about three hundred left in the world, all of them in the Gir Forest. It's a ways from here, but it's a restricted wildlife sanctuary. There aren't any outside Gir. Not on their own." Christian looked around the clearing, scanning the thick walls of plant life, looking for signs of a new threat. "Lions live and travel in prides. We'll have to be very careful. There may be more."

Brandon immediately split his attention between the lion and the jungle behind him.

"I can't believe his coloring." Christian eased forward and ran a tentative hand over the dead animal's dark, glistening fur. "He's nearly black. I've seen a few white ones in zoos, but never a black lion. He's incredible. "

Dragging his gaze off the perimeter, Brandon studied the sprawled lion, a new appreciation for its size and power settling in as his adrenaline levels finished spiking. Between the lack of caffeine and the tension, he was going to do a major crash and burn soon. He hoped it would wait until they got back to a comfortable hotel in a large city somewhere. One with room service, a hot tub in the room, and mattresses so thick he'd get lost in them.

"He's huge. Are all Asian lions this big?"

"No. He's at least a foot taller and a hundred pounds heavier than any lion I've ever seen. He must go six hundred pounds or more. He's utterly amazing."

"I'm almost sorry I shot him." Brandon glanced at Hari's body, then back to admire the beast. "Almost."

He stood up and walked over to the abandoned backpacks. "Let's get going." He glanced at their late guide's remains and grimaced at the flurry of insects that had already found the body. "It won't take long to bury him."

He shook his head to knock loose the image while he swung one of the packs onto his back and strapped down both the waist and chest belt. It was tightly packed with their remaining supplies. He knew this one had the coffee in it and he wasn't leaving it behind willingly.

With one last admiring look, Christian reluctantly rose from the lion and joined Brandon. Brandon propped his rifle against the nearest tree next to Christian's gun and helped the larger man struggle into the other, heavier pack. That's when all hell broke loose for the second time.

Without the slightest hint or warning, the dead lion sprang up off the ground. In one leap he came at them. The force of having six hundred pounds of muscle and bone launched at him sent Christian flying through the air to land twenty feet away from where he had been standing. Brandon watched him go down and stay down, a dazed look of surprise on his bloodied face.

Brandon didn't have time to see much else. His entire field of vision was taken up by teeth, whiskers, and thin black lips as a dark fury overtook him. He felt a searing stab of pain in his left shoulder so agonizing, his vision blacked out and his throat burned from the scream it forced out of his stunned lungs. A flip of the lion's head and Brandon's entire body flopped, his shoulder embedded between the beast's jaws. Suddenly the world moved as the big cat began to run, Brandon firmly gripped in his massive jaws, his arms and legs plummeting to the ground with each step and his head and face whipped by the thick underbrush.

His hands desperately clawed at the lion's mouth, hoping to cause enough pain that the cat would release him, even if only for a new grip. All Brandon understood now was making the animal let him go. His arm hit a tree trunk, turning it numb and useless. His fingers traced the pack's shoulder strap up into the animal's mouth, the heavy-duty webbing and thick canvas bag taking the weight of his body and keeping the sharp teeth in his shoulder from tearing out a sizable chunk of his flesh. His vision blurred again and the pain set him on fire. Brandon fumbled with the quick release clips with his usable hand, but with one vicious shake of the beast's head, the jungle went as dark as the cat's unnatural coat.

CHAPTER TEN

He could see most of the room from where he lay, but Brandon's vision played tricks with him and the room wavered and swayed if he moved his head too suddenly. It was cold, so very cold. Occasionally, when spasms of breath-stealing pain increased to a level so agonizing his entire body shook, the colors around him swirled, blending solid objects with sounds and smells to disorient him.

His arms were too heavy for him to lift, both of them in a continual state of burning pain. He thought his left arm was broken just above the wrist. His hand was numb and felt swollen. He couldn't even tell if his legs were still there. Every time he tried to lift his head to look, the pain in his lion-mauled shoulder hammered him back down and the world went black again.

This time, after two such failed attempts, he wanted to remain conscious. He needed to know more about where he was if he stood any hope of surviving. What good the information would be, he didn't know. He was still alive but he felt as if he'd been torn to shreds. Dried blood sealed his clothing to his raw flesh and stuck to his wounds, tugging agonizingly at tortured skin with each breath and movement.

His thoughts turned to his attacker and he wondered where the dark lion was now. Hiding in the shadows a few feet away, like he had been in the jungle, waiting, watching, and planning his move for when Brandon least expected it or was least prepared to defend himself? Right now he'd argue with anyone who told him a wild animal wasn't smart enough to stage an ambush. Christ, he'd have sworn that lion had been dead!

Moving his eyes more than his head, he slowly focused on his surroundings, taking in as much detail as possible, looking for escape routes and something to defend himself with if he even managed to move a body part other than his eyes.

Sputtering torches lit the room, dozens of them, all around him, each in carved stone holders fifteen feet up the walls. Shadows, long and dark, arched in the wide spaces between each torch, their fluid forms dancing with the flickering light. The room felt cavernous and dank. Humidity dripped from the vines, which grew in thick ropes down the walls and across the ceiling.

There was an underlying odor of animal smells in the air. Scurrying over the vines and sitting in various alcoves and ledges designed into the walls were dozens of small monkeys, some black and white, others a golden yellow. All of them made the same screeching, nerve-splitting cry Brandon had heard in the tree tops for the last day or so ever since they had begun the trek up the mountainside on the last leg of their journey.

The rich scent of jungle flowers told him it was night. The first night in the forest, Christian had presented him with a gorgeous plant that had reminded him of an orchid. The seasoned explorer had told him it bloomed only at night, like many of the jungle flowers, when the heat and torturous sun were gone.

Christian flashed into his mind and a cool sweat popped out on his flesh. He didn't know what had happen to his lover, but he was fairly certain he would never see Christian again. The man had few supplies left and was all alone in a murderous jungle surrounded by bloodthirsty wild animals. Maybe Christian had been right and there had been more lions lying in wait by the clearing.

The image of Christian's strong, handsome face stuck in his mind, forcing his chest to tighten and his eyes to water. Tears streamed freely down his temples, the salt in them stinging the open wounds he felt on his face as they trickled into his hair. He didn't bother to stop them. No one was here to see him cry and he didn't care if there was. He knew now he really loved Christian. He'd finally found someone he could see building a life with and in a heartbeat it was all gone, snatched away by a brutal twist of fate.

So much for a mystical adventure to find his heart's fucking desire. He should have stayed home, tossed the asshole Phil out on his ear, and started dating Christian. He'd have had the same thing he had now, but he would've actually been able to live to enjoy it.

He was fairly sure he was going to die here, if not right now, then soon. He'd lost a large amount of blood from his shoulder wound. He could feel it pooling under him and dripping down his skin. Passing out when he raised his head told him he was already shocky, and massive infection was probably already setting in. He was covered with dirt, grime, and probably lion drool. He didn't even try to keep the insects away from the drying blood. It would take too much energy and require him to raise his arms, which he couldn't do.

The sheen of sweat cooled on his skin and sent a shiver through him. He cried out, sudden nauseating pain reawakened, his voice echoing off the walls and high ceiling, ringing in his own ears and making him cringe. Surprisingly, the sound startled the troop of monkeys into silence. The monkeys stayed amazingly quiet, but a new voice filled the void.

"Bran-*don* is awake. Excellent."

The voice was feminine but strong, aristocratic and regal. It had a clipped lilt to it that made Brandon think of ancient Indian dynasties and old-fashioned, formal, book-learned British-accented English. It was exotic and seductive.

Faced with his obvious critical injuries, such a casual greeting was disconcerting. The woman was either blind or she didn't care he'd been savagely mauled by a lion and was bleeding to death. As she came into his field of vision, one glance at her smiling face and dancing eyes gave him his answer. The lady wasn't blind. But she was beautiful.

Her hair was midnight black, rolled in a bun worn low on the nape of her neck. A fan ornament sat atop her head with two metal cups attached to it, one at each temple. A long gold bangle hung from her left nostril, catching the light with every movement she made. Her sari was covered in bold print and color, and even her undergarments were patterned and vibrant, unlike the women Brandon had seen in the Indian villages and cities he'd visited so far. She was petite and delicate in stature, but there was an element of raw power and strength which radiated from her and made Brandon's skin turn to gooseflesh when she looked directly at him. Her eyes looked like lakes of black water, bottomless and cold.

"How do you know my name?"

The woman raised her hand and a small, dove-gray bird flew down from somewhere above them. It landed on her finger, squawked a few familiar notes, and took off again. Brandon recognized the splash of white on its beak and face as his jungle companion, the babbler.

She smiled coyly. "A little bird told me."

"Where am I?" He was surprised at the weakness in his voice. It was so soft that he could hardly hear it himself. She, however, didn't have any trouble hearing him from twenty feet away and closing.

"A man who asks questions instead of trying to run. The pale-skinned men who venture here, all to obtain the sacred statue of Karttikeya as you have undoubtedly come for, are often more talkative than the local peasants. I am pleased." Her gaze raked over his body and Brandon shivered at the coldness in it. "I enjoy a little dinner conversation before a meal."

She wasn't making any sense to him, but he blamed his pain and blood loss. He could feel blood trickling out of his shoulder wound where the lion had grabbed him. It pooled under his back, a cold, jellied mess. He could smell the old congealed blood mixing with the new.

"Who... are you?" Waves of dizziness struck and his vision spun, making her measured approach look like a floating ball of brilliant color coming to him.

"I am Kamat, guardian of this temple, the sacred temple of Karttikeya."

"You're the guardian of the temple?" Gaze traveling over her tiny frame and delicate features, he couldn't keep the surprise off his face. "You don't look like the *mande burung* the men were frightened of."

"I am not." She walked to his side.

The table came to her waist and he realized he was lying on was some type of altar, with symbols carved around the edges. She bent low, hovering close to his face and Brandon saw the tips of fangs extending from her delicate, full-lipped mouth. White tips glistened in the torchlight and stood out stark against her dark skin.

"I am a creature more fearsome and deadly than he could ever be." The way she said it, Brandon believed her.

A dark shadow behind Kamat rippled forward. As light hit the shadow, the dark lion emerged, his sable coat blending seamlessly with the blackness. Brandon cringed and froze, air locked in his paralyzed lungs. When the lion remained impassively at Kamat's side, Brandon started breathing again.

"I'd argue with you, lady, but I'm not in any position to scoff at your ability to do damage." He glanced at the lion. "Or have it done." He gasped, pain shuddering through his torn and gaping shoulder wound. The massive beast growled, then nuzzled Kamat's neck and licked her cheek. She buried her hands in his thick mane like a lover's embrace. "He's a pet?"

"He is much more than that, but it is of no concern to you. Your time is almost over." She stroked a tattooed hand over the exposed side of Brandon's neck, fingers rubbing the length of his rapidly pulsing artery. Brandon could feel his heartbeat in the firm pressure of her touch.

She bared her fangs and Brandon had no illusions he was going to survive her attack. The lion had almost done him in. He was maimed, broken, and bleeding to death. If this woman actually tore his throat out with her sharpened teeth, he didn't stand a chance of living through another savage bloodfest, but he didn't have the strength to move a muscle to avoid her before she struck.

She rubbed her smooth dark bronze cheek over his jaw, making the abrasions and cuts on his skin burn and throb. She nuzzled his neck and actually licked the skin over his pulse, ignoring the dirt, blood, and sweat on his flesh.

"You should be spending the moments you have left remembering all you will leave behind." Her voice was soft and breathy, but one look in her black eyes and Brandon knew she was the embodiment of death.

"If you're going to kill me, why are you talking with me?"

"I have few guests that are willing to do more than scream. I find I miss conversation. As I said, I prefer a little dinner conversation before a meal." Kamat smiled and licked Brandon's artery again. He saw a stain of his own blood on her lips as she slowly lapped it off with her tongue. A look of pure lust and need lit up her face. "Even if it is *with* my meal."

"W-what?" As unbelievable as it was, he suddenly suspected her fanged teeth weren't filed to points as part of a bizarre, secret blood cult like he had originally thought.

"I am *churel*."

She made the word sound exotic, dark, and threatening. But that was all "churel" meant to Brandon. He gave her an uncomprehending stare. Her smile sent chills down his spine.

"Vam-*pyre* in your modern world."

"What the . . . ? You're a *vampire*?" He knew he was in shock because he believed her. He didn't know why, but all the odd happenings like the babbler and the reanimation of the dead lion made him instinctively understand this *was* possible here in this primitive world. But, damn, he wasn't giving up without a fight. He was in too much pain from his current life-threatening injuries to care about one more hurt.

"*Bite me!*" It may not have been the best choice of words, but it was meant in sarcasm as a small defiance. Unfortunately, she seemed to take him literally.

Baring her fangs, Kamat leaned in close and laughed, her fingers continuing to trail down Brandon's pounding artery, her caress to his neck becoming more and more firm, nails biting into his flesh. Small beads of blood welled up in the scratches. Brandon's flinched at the new pain, but shuddered when the woman lunged forward and bit his neck.

Her teeth sliced the first few layers of flesh, then she withdrew them, satisfying herself by sucking at the fresh wound with a force that told Brandon he would have a bruise in the shape of her mouth there. His heartbeat fluttered in his throat, irregular and weak, a wave of dizziness washing over him. Only a few seconds passed before she pulled away, a wet sucking sound filling the chamber, disappointment clearly written on her face.

"Your heart falters." His blood was dark, a brilliant, glistening red against the paler bronze of her lips. It stained her once bright white teeth and fangs, the sight making Brandon nauseous. "I cannot enjoy my meal this way. I would have you strong." Kamat raised her arm and bit into the soft flesh. As the blood ran, she forced her arm into Brandon's mouth and held it there.

Startled, Brandon tried to twist away, too weak and in too much pain to do more than turn his head, and even that small effort made the room dip and sway in a dangerous manner. He felt like he was falling off the altar into a bottomless whirlpool of swirling colors and screeching, inhuman sounds.

The attempt to disengage the woman's arm was useless; her strength far surpassed his. He suspected it would be that way even if he had been healthy. Blood filled his mouth and blocked his airway, his head held immobile by an iron hand clamped to his jaw. He held his breath for as long as he could, then relented and swallowed, the blood cool and thick, coating his throat and curdling in his stomach. The taste of copper, metallic and bitter, brought a grimace to his bruised and scratched face, awakening a new set of aches.

After he'd gulped down two full mouthfuls, Kamat removed her arm. Brandon felt a trickle of coolness roll from the corner of his mouth, but he was loath to catch it with his tongue. Kamat leaned down to whisk it off his skin with her agile tongue, eyes wide and shining brightly in the torchlight.

The monkeys chattered louder, swinging down from the ledges and vines to screech warnings, tiny paws pulling at the white tufts on their ears, the small golden-yellow ones tucked tight to breasts or riding on hunched backs, visible now as youngsters. A low, disgruntled growl and heavy breathing came from the pacing lion, the disgruntled sound impatient, almost like he resented being left out of the meal.

Her blood settled in the pit of Brandon's stomach, heavy and cold enough to make him shiver. It mixed with the curdling stomach acids. Suddenly, heat burned his belly, scorching and painful, threads of white lightning shooting out to race along his overstimulated nerves, leaving them abused and tingling with pain.

With the pain came a new kind of strength, a lessening of his exhaustion, a dulling of the agony of his maimed shoulder and bruised, torn, and broken limbs. His heart beat a little stronger and his breathing eased. It would have been a relief, if it hadn't come with the knowledge this *vampire* had partially healed him in order to inflict more damage and pain on him.

Kamat's fingers danced over his neck again, the flesh tender and bruised, hypersensitive to her fleeting touch. "That is much better. I prefer not to have to hang you from the ceiling to draw out your blood."

She leaned in close once again, hand gripping Brandon's jaw, hold tighter than before. Drawing back for a plunging attack, fangs bared and lips pulled back in a death grimace, Kamat poised for her final kill.

Brandon froze, panic in his eyes, lungs and limbs paralyzed. He closed his eyes and willed the image of Christian to rise up behind his eyelids, wanting his lover to be the last thing he saw, not the twisted mask of this supernatural murderess.

"I wouldn't do that if I were you."

His lover's voice cut through the air, crisp, clear, and unexpected. Brandon immediately thought he had blacked out and missed her attack until the restraining hand moved from his jaw to grip his hair. The pain from the hold was sharp and harsh, forcing him to open his eyes.

Christian crouched low by a far wall to Brandon's left, a rappelling rope in one hand. His other hand gripped a large bore handgun that he trained on Kamat.

"Let go and step away from him."

Brandon caught Christian's eye and the man gave him a wink and an encouraging smile, then hurriedly resumed dividing his attention between Kamat and the massive lion who had prowled toward the archaeologist before Christian's feet had hit the ground.

"Bullets will not harm me, human," Kamat hissed at Christian, disdain and fury flowing around her like an almost visible cloak.

"This gun doesn't shoot bullets, lady. It shoots flares. Fire bullets. It'll explode in your chest and set you on fire in a heartbeat. If you had one. I've got enough flares for your friend there, too."

"I control you here, human. You have been under my influence since you made your camp last night. I called you to that clearing and I welcomed you into my house from there." She gestured at the room, indicating the ancient temple in her description of her "home." "I believe you found my invitation, a clay cup like this one, in the clearing."

Christian nodded, his hand automatically brushing the pocket that contained the broken shard. "I found what was left of one, a single piece of broken pottery, yes."

"Yet it was enough to bring you to me."

"The brightly patterned mix of designs and color in your clothing and nose jewelry are distinctive. I've seen them before. And the circular tattoos at your temples. They can only mean one thing. You're from the Banjara gypsy bands, aren't you? In southern India. That's why all the monkeys and the Persian lion are here." Christian swept an arm through the air above his head, making the troops of hyper monkeys screech and jump in place at the attention. "You brought them to be with you, to make this your 'home'."

"After untold centuries in this barren place, we missed our lands and the creatures that dwell within them. Ahmedabad--" She tilted her head to indicate the dark lion. "--and I are wanderers. Since we no longer roam freely, our familiars came to us."

"Your people have a great respect for guests, if I remember correctly, don't they?" Christian didn't answer. Kamat merely glared at him, her eyes blazing each time her unblinking stare moved to the gun in his hand.

Christian studied the mismatched pair of captors. His eyes narrowed, mouth set in a grim line of concentration. Brandon could tell the archaeologist was searching for an advantage over the situation. He learned early during the trip that Christian was a detail person, always studying and planning, formulating options and alternate means of accomplishing things. Brandon had listed it as one of the scientist's mildly irritating quirks, but now he was glad the man was so damn meticulous, always thinking. Brandon's cop skills weren't going to get them past this point. His gun was gone, he was flat on his back bleeding to death, and his brain could barely function with any amount of clarity.

"The Banjara are an ancient culture from as far back as the tenth century. They had strict rules and customs about inviting strangers to their home, didn't they? If I remember it correctly--" Christian took the found pottery shard out of his vest pocket and pressed it into the palm of his hand. "--no invited visitor may be harmed while in a Banjara home."

He jumped up onto the edge of the altar. Awkward with one hand, Christian gently picked Brandon's shoulders up until he could kneel behind his lover. The flare gun never lowered, moving from target to target keeping both Kamat and her lion at bay.

"Christian! Christ! Ahhhh! Fuck! Damn!" Brandon gritted his teeth and cursed to keep from screaming too loudly. The muted sound still echoed off the chamber walls and sent the monkeys into a new round of chattering frenzy. Even the dark lion roared his displeasure at the distressing noise.

"I'm sorry, Brandon, so sorry, babe." Christian kissed Brandon's head and wrapped his arms around him, supporting the wounded man's upper body with his chest and open thighs as he knelt close behind him.

The warmth from Christian's body was blissful and unexpected. Brandon sighed and tried to force himself to relax back into Christian's embrace. It was probably the last one they would share, so he wanted to experience every moment of it. More urgent kisses peppered his hair and neck before Christian pulled him closer and turned his attention back to Kamat.

"You may have lured us into a trap with this--" Christian opened his hand and revealed the pottery shard, its sharp edges having dug into his palm enough to make it bleed. "--but you also welcomed us into your home with it at the same time." A trickle of bright red oozed around its pointed ends.

The slow, seductive way Kamat licked her lips at the sight of it made Brandon's blood run cold. A purely animalistic light shone behind her half-lidded eyelids. Coupled with the pearl-white fang tips, she looked as deadly as she claimed to be.

Christian grabbed Brandon's left hand.

"The other arm, other arm!" Brandon's voice was strained and urgent. "This side isn't working so hot."

Christian immediately let go. He grabbed Brandon's skinned and bruised right hand and entwined their fingers in a tight grasp, the broken shard pressed between their hands. "You also have to honor the rest of the custom. The protection extends to all in my household."

Kamat smiled a sly, tolerant smile that reminded Brandon of a cat who had cornered a mouse. "Very clever. You two are by far the most interesting travelers we have had here in all the years I have guarded this temple and its sacred statue. But the Banjara pledge of protection extends only to your spouse and offspring, Chris-*ti*-an." She made his name sound sinful and exotic, the syllables rolling off her tongue like a snake's hiss.

"Mere lovers do not count. The gods do not accept the oblation of a bachelor."

Kamat began walking slowly around the room as she talked, the dark lion remaining rooted to the spot in front of the altar. It forced Christian to swerve back and forth to keep either of them from getting too close.

"I can fix that." Christian nudged Brandon with his chin, whispering into his ear low and urgent. "You still with me, Brandon? You awake, babe?"

"Uh-huh. I'm 'wake." He felt his head roll to one side, his cheek resting on the coarse canvas of Christian's vest. It smelt like campfire smoke and Christian's sweat. It brought back memories of the taste of his lover's skin and the feel of his body under his hands. Brandon smiled, liking the idea that this would be one of his last conscious thoughts.

"Good."

Brandon was jostled again, a little harder. The pain made him pull his head up and focus on Christian's voice.

"Repeat after me. Don't question it, just do it, Brandon. And fast. Okay?"

Christian's constant swaying arm movement to keep Kamat and the lion in his sights was making Brandon nauseous, but the jarring pain it caused kept him awake. He muttered, "'Kay, 'kay. So talk to me."

"*Your heart is in mine and mine is in yours.*" Christian's words were rushed, grunted out rather than recited.

"Your heart is in mine... and mine is in... yours." Brandon's words were more gasped than spoken.

"*I will never leave you nor forsake you; I will spend all my days at your side.*"

"I will never leave you… nor forsake you." Brandon bit back a moan, grimaced and blinked several times to try to keep his eyes open and focused. "I'll spend all my days at your goddamned side." He groaned, a small sob unexpectedly rising up from his chest. Under his breath he added, "It'll be a short visit, Chris."

"No improvising." Christian squeezed Brandon's hand. The points of the pottery piece jabbed into his palm, the pain forcing him to stay focused. "*We will share a lifetime of eternal, immeasurable love.*"

"Lifetime. Eternal, immeasurable love." Brandon's strength was fading along with his ability to stay conscious.

Christian nudged his head again hard, speaking desperately into Brandon's ear, voice tense, and with a touch of panic in it. The panic made Brandon try harder to stay alert. He saw Christian's gun arm start to tremble and he realized even Christian was nearing his physical limits on this unholy quest.

Kamat stopped pacing and stared, the frown on her beautiful face turning into surprise when she recognized the words. "You cannot be serious," she scoffed, dismissing the ancient ritual verse, but her narrowed eyes showed signs of irritated betrayal. "There is no priest here to perform *saptapadi.*"

"Don't need a priest. You know that. Just two consenting partners." Christian prompted Brandon with a kiss to his neck, his warm breath scalding Brandon's skin. "Come on babe, one more." He gripped Brandon's hand harder. "*You have become mine forever. I have become yours. We are word and meaning, united.*"

"Words and meaning united? What the hell is that?"

"Say it! *You have become mine --*"

"Okay, okay. You have become mine forever. I have become yours. We are word and meaning, united."

Christian slowly lowered the gun. Neither Kamat nor the lion approached them. Instead, Kamat stalked to the animal's side and stood glaring at them. Bodies plastered together, Brandon could hear and feel the relief flow through his partner.

Brandon rolled his head to see Christian's grime-smeared face. "That's it? We're married?"

"You got it. You're stuck with me now. A sacred vow in the temple of Karttikeya, one of the few Hindu gods who wasn't interested in women. How appropriate is that?"

What little strength he had regained through Kamat's blood was waning. He wanted to share one more thing with Christian before it disappeared for good. "A traditional temple wedding. Who'd have guessed? Do you get to kiss the bride now?"

"It's not a done deal until we do." Christian smiled, pleasure lighting up his face that could be seen even through the layers of sweat and dirt he wore.

"Then make it official. It's bad form to keep the bride waiting."

The kiss was sweet, deep, and long. Brandon poured all his pent-up emotions into it. He could feel Christian's heated response answer him in kind. For a brief moment, his pain dulled, his senses overwhelmed by Christian's love and the gnawing ache of regret for the life he would never get to experience with this amazing man. He pulled back and let his head fall to Christian's shoulder, taking comfort in the man's warmth and the strength of his arms around him. If he had to die, wrapped in Christian's embrace wasn't such a bad way to go, all things considered.

"I cannot harm you while you are here, but--" Kamat smiled. "--I do not have to let you leave. I can keep you here until you starve to death." She slowly advanced on the couple, a curious look on her face, her eyes darting from Christian to

Brandon, her critical gaze clearly evaluating the men's physical attributes. "Or..."

"Or?" Christian frowned as she circled the table, eyeing them like animals at an auction.

"You two are not like the others who have come here before on their quest to be granted riches and fame by the sacred statue. Your quest for the statue comes from the heart, as was mine when I first sought out the power of Karttikeya. In over nine hundred years, only one other pair of lovers has attempted to possess the statue. They failed, as you have failed. But your love for each other appears strong. Each of you has risked pain and death to defend and protect the other. I wish to witness this love."

"Witness it?" Christian exchanged a guarded look with Brandon. He asked incredulously, "Like in *watch*?"

"My existence has been a lonely one. My love is... unattainable for me." Her eyes flashed a dark red hue. Her gaze grew sultry and intense. "I wish to *experience* you and yours."

Her gaze now felt like a caress and Brandon felt his cock stir. Danger had always been a turn-on for him, but he was surprised to have his tormented body react at this moment.

"Lady, in case you hadn't noticed, Brandon is not in any condition for anything more physical than a helicopter airlift out to a hospital. You've also seemed to miss the thrust of the relationship here between the two of us. The spirit of the wedding vows was real. Neither of us is physically attracted to women. That might make it a little tough to let you 'experience' us."

"I am vampyre." The phrase was spit out, regal and disdainful, a queen explaining royalty to an uneducated peasant. "Although we still enjoy physical mating, vampyres make love through their other senses. I can experience your lovemaking and emotions through a blood link without being an active participant in the act."

"Blood link?"

"You taste a sip of my blood, I take a sip of yours. It is simple. My blood will link you with me. The effects last only a short time."

Brandon gestured at the pools of his blood bathing the altar. He meant to wave his arm, but the only body part that responded was a single finger. He sighed and tapped the stone slab beneath him. His whole body was going numb, the pain receding to a distant ache. "I think you've gotten all the blood from me I can spare, Kamat. So sorry."

She ignored him and stared at Christian. "You are now head of your household. The decision rests with you. I already forged a blood link with your... spouse."

Brandon couldn't believe it when Christian paused, obviously thinking over the suggestion. "Chris?" It came out a lot weaker than his voice had been just a few moments ago.

"Give me a minute." Christian kissed Brandon's unbruised cheek quick and hard, then tightened both arms around Brandon's shivering torso. "What do we get out of this?"

Kamat huffed and waved a hand in disdain. "To live?"

"Including Brandon?"

"His injuries are of little concern." Her contempt dripped from her voice, her glance half-lidded and bored.

"Maybe to you." Brandon gave a snorted, mirthless chuckle and closed his eyes. It was taking all his energy just to focus on the conversation. He knew it was important, but he was having trouble caring.

"They can be healed. The power of eternal life flows in my veins." Kamat flashed her fangs. "I am over one thousand years old."

"What about the statue we came for?" Brandon interrupted. If there was a chance they could get out of here, Brandon wanted to know what the odds of completing their goal were. He'd bled for this damn statue.

"It remains here. I am still guardian." Kamat left no doubt that there was no compromise here.

Christian jumped back into the negotiations, fast and furious. "But you'll heal Brandon completely, let us live, *and* let us go?"

"Yes." This time the word was accompanied by a sultry stare as Kamat discarded her outer sash, the move seductive and blatant.

"So if we agree to let you watch us make love--" Christian pressed a hand to Brandon's shoulder, his palm coming away bright with fresh blood, the wound torn open during the earlier effort to move Brandon. "--you'll heal Brandon, right now, and let us go free?"

"Yes." It was a long, drawn-out word that ended in an ominous hiss.

"Okay. We'll do it."

CHAPTER ELEVEN

"Chris?"

Brandon shuddered as increasing coldness invaded his body. His bones ached, his wounds throbbed, and his limbs had grown too heavy to lift again. Every breath Christian took, every slight movement he made, was transmitted through the tight embrace Christian held him in, jarring him. It was an agonizing comfort. Brandon didn't see how anything, mystical or not, could heal his injuries.

"I'm all for getting naked with you, lover, but I don't think I'm going to live that long." Brandon gasped as a shooting pain squeezed his chest, the pressure so great it felt like his spine was being crushed to his sternum. "I need a doctor, not... whatever she is."

The room was already darker and colder, his hearing muted and his vision blurred and distorted. It was almost a relief to block Kamat, the lion, the blood-soaked altar, and the pain. Unfortunately, it was taking Christian away, too, and that was the last thing he wanted to happen.

"It's okay, Brandon, trust me on this." Christian slowly scrambled around on his knees, turning until Brandon lay in his arms and over his lap, making it easier to see him face to face. He supported Brandon's upper torso with his thighs and one arm under Brandon's shoulders. Mercifully avoiding the worst of the cuts and abrasions Brandon had suffered by being dragged through the jungle by Ahmedabad, he caressed the side of Brandon's face.

Christian spoke low and urgently, as if he understood there wasn't much time left to them. "I don't trust her, but I believe her. I know the legends about her people. If she really is a churel, she can heal you."

Brandon gave him a disbelieving stare, the only thing he had any energy left to do.

Dividing his attention between Brandon, then Kamat and the lion -- to make sure they weren't going to try anything -- Christian leaned down and pecked a fast furious kiss to Brandon's colorless lips. "Trust me. Just trust me, okay?"

Blinking hard to focus on Christian's face, Brandon gave a weak smile. Christian looked worried and exhausted, covered in sweat, jungle grime and Brandon's blood. He looked stunning to Brandon, handsome and stalwart, like an adventure hero in the movies. He was so glad he'd had the chance to have this man in his life, even for a short while, before his life was over.

Brandon nodded. "I never could say no to a good-looking guy. I trust you." Then he haltingly added, "Love you, too." He grimaced, trying to smile through a spasm of pain. "Needed to say that, in case this doesn't work."

The love he saw in Christian's face grew and turned more determined.

"Love you, too. I'm going to show you just how much as soon as you're feeling better."

Christian slowly laid Brandon down on the stone altar and slid his arm out from under him. Brandon immediately missed the warmth and the reassuring pressure, feeling like he had lost a tangible link to the living with its withdrawal. Christian moved back to sit at his side, hand resting lightly on Brandon's hip. Brandon could feel the weight of his lover's palm, even if he was too numb to sense the heat.

"We'll get through this together," Christian firmly added. Brandon could only nod again. Right hand trembling with the effort to reach Christian's hand on his hip, his fingers didn't get off the cold stone slab before they were clutched tightly in Christian's hand. Again, he felt the sharp edges of the pottery shard against his flesh, this time the sensation muted and indistinct.

Suddenly, a new touch startled him, cold and firm, gripping his injured shoulder. He glanced over his head to see Kamat standing over him. The tattered remains of his shirt were peeled away from the raw, savage wound and torn from his body in one vicious yank, exposing his chest and jarring his broken arm. He screamed at the pain, but all that came out was a feeble moan. The woman's strength was unreal, supporting her claim of supernatural powers. If the pain hadn't been so blindingly horrible, the act almost made Brandon appreciate the possibility that her powers were real.

"Look at me, Bran-*don*." Sharp nails trailed over his skin from his neck, across his mangled shoulder and down his broken arm to tap impatiently on the palm of his useless left hand.

Kamat had moved down the altar to stand beside him, a hypnotic expression of pure lust and power radiating from her so strongly she seemed to shimmer in the flaring firelight. Brandon blinked, his gaze captured in her dark stare. Within seconds he felt himself relax, but his eyes stayed fixed on Kamat's face, unable to tear his gaze away from hers. He slumped, even his fingers in Christian's grip going still and lifeless. His tongue and lips worked, but no sound escaped them. Christian wordlessly squeezed his slack hand tighter.

Kamat held a clay cup, simple in form, oversized and thick-walled, but ornate in adornment and color, and obviously very, very old. The colors reminded Brandon of the pottery shard Christian now pressed into his hand. The colors and design were similar, and he fleetingly wondered what the symbols on it meant. He hadn't cared before, but now it seemed to matter. Everything had significance and hidden meaning, all directed at him at the moment. But he couldn't think clearly and Kamat wasn't giving him time to linger over anything.

"A sacred chalice from days long gone from this world. It has held the blood of some of the greatest beings in existence from both your world and mine." She spun it slowly in her hand, admiringly, showing both men the symbols engraved in the sides. "Four symbols depict the elements of nature – earth, wind, fire, and water, and the fifth--" She turned the chalice so that a symbol that looked like a horned cross could be seen. "--belongs to a world so secret, so ancient, few who live in your world have ever seen it and remained in the light. My world."

A chill invaded his bones and Brandon shuddered, the icy finality in her voice and her stare leeching any remaining warmth from him. He knew the only thing holding him to this life was Christian's own death grip on his hand. It was a slim tether to his quickly fading mortal existence.

Silent again, Kamat slashed open her own arm above the wrist and swiftly and expertly collected the dark, thick blood into the ceremonial cup. When the blood ceased to flow by itself, she extended the same arm and made a clicking sound in the back of her throat. Immediately, one of the monkeys disengaged itself from the troop to swing down to land on her raised upper arm and shoulder.

The remainder of the troop began a muttered chatter that rose and fell, the inhuman singsong rhythm echoing off the walls and ceiling, rolling into a chanting wave within seconds. It was eerie, sending a shiver of unease though Brandon.

Ahmedabad moved several paces to be nearer Kamat's side, his cold, expressionless gaze never leaving her.

It was a large monkey with white tufts on its thighs and long, wavy white strands of hair growing from behind its small ears. It screeched softly, periodically tugging at the bun of inky black hair that extended out the back of Kamat's headpiece. It anxiously shifted from sitting to a crouched standing position and back again until Kamat allowed the monkey to curl around her slashed forearm. Then she cradled it to her chest, blood cup still in her other hand.

"She is a lutung, the Nilgiri Langur breed. Do you know them, Chris-*ti*-an?"

The archaeologist nodded, reluctantly studying the monkey. But Brandon could see a new light in his eyes. Always the scientist, even now. "Yes, I do know about them. They're thought to be extinct. Poached to non-existence for the aphrodisiac properties their organs are said to contain."

Kamat nodded, fingers curled into the animal's fur. "It is true, their blood-engorged organs can enhance a lover's intimacy, but their true power lies only within their blood. It can heal and restore, granting vitality and strength." She turned the monkey so its back was facing her. The animal's beady little eyes darted from Brandon and Christian. "When mixed with the power of a churel's blood, the effects are magnified and accelerated a hundredfold." She tucked the monkey under her chin and smiled arrogantly. "Especially blood as old and knowledgeable as mine."

Without warning, Kamat sank her fangs into the monkey's back, face buried in the black fur so closely that Brandon couldn't see her expression. The monkey flinched, but otherwise remained unnaturally still and silent, clinging to Kamat's arm with all four limbs, mouth partially open and a glazed look on its tiny expressive face.

Kamat released the monkey with a soothing pat to its flank before it scurried away, and spat her mouthful of its blood into the cup. Unexpectedly, a wisp of red mist became visible above the lip of the cup as it rose up into the air. Kamat inhaled it and the vapors disappeared, drawn into her lungs and, by the expression on her face, savored like the finest opium smoke.

Brandon felt Christian's fingers on his wrist, the pressure from them suddenly harsh. He couldn't turn his head to look at his lover, but Christian's voice was low and anxious, making Brandon picture the man with a worried frown on his handsome face.

"I'm losing his pulse, Kamat."

Her expression turned sultry, something dark and terrifying in it. Brandon found it disturbing and yet thrilling, her surreal power radiating off her like heat, repelling and attracting him at the same time. He watched her lick the ring of blood from her lips like it was the sweetest ambrosia, hands gripping the cup, gently swirling the contents.

Eyes heavy-lidded, tinged with red with no discernible pupils in their inky depths, she bared her pink-tinged fangs and hissed, "It is time."

"Wait. I--"

Apparently, Brandon's open mouth had been all she had been waiting for. Raising the cup, she forced the edge between Brandon's jaws and poured the mixture down his throat, stopping when there was only a mouthful of the putrid concoction left.

Brandon gagged and choked, fighting the vile-tasting substance, its slick, clinging texture coating his mouth, tongue, and throat in a thick gelatinous layer. He struggled not to swallow, then found himself convulsively doing it to rid himself of the foul taste. As each mouthful made its way to his stomach, Brandon felt it lurch in protest, the resulting spasms reawakening the pain. Then suddenly the spasms relaxed and Brandon felt a strangely euphoric sensation in his gut. It expanded until he thought he could feel every molecule in his body. In his mind's eye, he could see the blood he had swallowed infusing every organ and cell. He was numb, tingling, and flushed all at once. His head spun and the room swirled with it.

Brandon's perception of the archaic, primitive setting suddenly became sharper, more defined and surreal. The stone chamber grew more exotic and mysterious, the torchlight becoming almost blindingly brilliant. The huge blocks of what had been sections of stone pillars strewn here and there took on the forms of ancient sentries, exotic and still. The irrefutable knowledge that the stone slab beneath his bare back was a sacred altar, bloodied by thousands of human offerings and possessing a frightening power of its own, seeped into his brain as his body absorbed the blood. His eyes were riveted to Kamat's stare, the whites of her eyes disappearing to be replaced by all black, turning them into glassy orbs of fathomless shadows. He felt like he was seeing more than any mere man should know.

Brandon could see himself in their depths like a reflection on a pool of oil. He looked beaten and battered, flesh torn and missing from his body, skin past pale to ashen gray, left arm misshapen, legs sprawled, bare chest bathed in a sickening combination of dry and fresh blood that painted his skin like nightmarish tattoos. His face was a checkerboard of slashes, intermingled with swollen bruises. A few cuts were scabbed over at the corners while others remained raw and gaping, but dry, even the flesh beneath the openings pale and bloodless now.

His heart fluttered in his chest and Brandon expected it to stop when it gave a thunderous stuttering few beats and paused. His chest froze, and he was unable to draw in a single breath. All strength leeched out of him and he wished desperately he could turn away from Kamat's hypnotic hold to look at Christian one last time, hoping the full extent of love and respect his heart harbored for this courageous man would show in his face during these last moments.

A flash of something terrifying, nightmarish, exploded in Kamat's eyes, the rippling waves of its power traveling directly to Brandon's paralyzed organs. A liquid fire, agonizingly bright and scorching hot, erupted along his spine. It spread out in all directions using his collapsed, nearly empty blood vessels as a highway, tracing the path Kamat's blood cocktail had taken.

The fire snapped and sparked, scalding its way through his body, making him jerk and writhe. He could feel his bones creaking as they knit, hear his flesh regenerating, the sound like the crackling of old newspaper thrown in a blazing hearth, his cuts closing with a sickly sucking sound and his swollen bruises fading away with a rush that made his skin felt singed and tender. It was horrifically painful and exhilarating. He felt reborn.

Chest abruptly heaving, air swooped into Brandon's lungs and his heart gave another thunderous beat. A strong steady rhythm stumbled to life once more, thumping under his repaired rib cage. Sensation returned to his limbs, and this time, it was not searing pain. Exhausted, skin tingling with an uncomfortable tenderness, Brandon realized he felt whole again.

He had to make an effort to adjust his gaze. It was still locked on Kamat's intense, frightening stare, but everything around him had fallen into a blurry mix of color and shape. It took a huge amount of concentration for Brandon to bring the room and its occupants back into sharp focus. As soon as he did, he found he could blink again and he turned to look at Christian, relieved he could now move freely, if a bit weary.

He was surprised when Kamat allowed him to pull away from her hold, but he didn't question it. Instead, he squeezed the hand still tightly gripping his own and gave Christian a weak, but delighted and somewhat shell-shocked, smile.

"Hey." The stunned look on Christian's face put Brandon at a loss for words. He studied the mix of horror and amazement on his lover's face and suddenly wondered if he looked differently than before the lion attack -- if Kamat had rearranged his face along with healing his maimed body. "Is it okay? Do I look the same?"

Nodding, Christian stared at Brandon, gaze running over and over him, taking in the healed wounds and bruises and mended bones. Awe competed with delight until both filled his voice.

"You look... I think I just witnessed..." Christian gestured helplessly with one hand, the other still clutching Brandon's. "...either a miracle or magic." He let out a long breath and blinked rapidly for a few seconds as if the action would help clear his mind as well as his sight. "I'm having trouble believing my eyes. I've heard of this being done, read about it once in an ancient text, but I never thought I'd actually see it."

He stared at Brandon anew and Brandon could see scientific wonder pushing the awe a little to one side. "It was horrible and amazing at the same time. I can't *really* explain it." Christian tentatively touched Brandon's cheek. Brandon flinched slightly at the touch. It felt like Christian had caressed a mildly raw spot on his skin.

"I'm just glad it happened. Miracle, magic, black or white, I'm just happy to have you back alive and--" He touched Brandon's left shoulder, now covered with new flesh and skin. "--whole again."

Leaning down, he kissed Brandon hungrily, love and relief mingling with passion and need. Brandon felt his cock harden, danger, renewed life and Christian's voracious embrace overwhelming him. He felt consumed by lust and eager to share his passion with the one man who had shown himself to be everything Brandon could hope for in a lover -- loyal, brave, intelligent, and resourceful. He could even forgive Christian's earnest nagging about his excessive coffee intake and addiction to Sparkles candy.

Brandon gave himself completely to the kiss, his hands, lips, and tongue diving into it, his soul overwhelmed by the realization he was being given a second chance at life. A second chance at love with Christian. A second chance that had been granted him by... a vampire.

The reminder that Kamat was there, watching and waiting in the shadows, made Brandon jerk back from Christian, his eyes darting immediately to the churel. Somehow he knew exactly where she was without having seen her.

Before, he only thought of her "that woman," and then a few other less charitable names, but "churel" was the only word that came to mind for her now. Her blood was in his veins, her presence in his mind, and he truly knew she was all she had claimed she was. It was terrifying, but strangely erotic to him. Much like Christian had said about witnessing his healing, it was impossible to explain, but when she spoke, he heard her in his head as well as with his ears.

"To fulfill the bargain, you will also need to drink, Chris-*ti*-an."

Her voice was now husky and thick, her exotic accent more hypnotic with each word. She came close to the edge of the altar, a more fluid, graceful step to her bearing, and she held the clay cup once more, offering it to Christian. Her eyes were still solid orbs of black, but a flash of red highlighted them every time the torchlight reflected in them. Her expression was sultry, full of anticipation and burning lust. Ahmedabad had moved to her side, his own fierce expression and massive features somehow mirroring Kamat's emotions. Brandon tried to block that thought out of his mind, but he had the fleeting impression the animal was as connected to him as Kamat was now.

Exchanging a smoldering glance with Brandon, Christian grabbed the cup from her hands, but as he looked down at the remaining blood concoction, he hesitated.

Brandon nodded and touched his arm encouragingly. "Go ahead. It tastes like crap, but no worse than cheap coffee that's been on the burner for over ten hours." Brandon surprised both of them with a chuckle. "God, I'm hopeless. That actually sounds good."

"Caffeine addict." It was said softly tolerant, Christian's voice affectionate and low.

"You think?" Brandon sat up and encouraged Christian to drink. "The first thing we do when we get out of this is..." He paused and reconsidered, giving Christian a heated look of need and desire. "Okay, scratch that. The *second* thing we do when we get out of this is find a party-size coffee urn for the kitchen."

"Your kitchen or mine?" The corners of Christian's eyes crinkled, weather-beaten and tanned when he smiled like that. Brandon liked that playful smile a lot.

"Ours." He pushed the cup to his lover's lips. "Now drink before I come from just watching you swallow." He'd lowered his voice for the last statement, but Brandon didn't think it mattered. He was sure Kamat knew everything he was thinking since he'd drunk from the cup anyway. His gaze followed the cup to Christian's lips and he lingered over the long arch of Christian's throat as he tipped the cup back and slugged down the mixture in one gulp.

Still on his knees beside Brandon, Christian swayed and blinked several times. Brandon knew the room was shifting and perceptions were twisting in an unsettling manner for Christian. He stayed seated on the massive stone slab, one hand resting reassuringly on Christian's thigh. After less than thirty seconds, he heard Kamat sigh, the lion rumble in response, and Christian dropped his chin to his chest. When he raised his head, the fire and need in his stare pulled Brandon up to his knees so he was chest to chest with Christian.

Chapter Twelve

Brandon ignored the uncomfortably hard surface under his knees. His hands traced over Christian's shoulders and upper arms, the solid muscle and flesh assuring him Christian was real.

"How did you find me?" Bright passion filled gazes locked together, hunger and need pushing aside normal considerations. Brandon felt Christian's hands grip his waist, the fingers digging into his skin just above his waistband. His naked chest was crushed to Christian's coarse, multi-pocketed vest and cotton work shirt. The heavy fabric and metal snaps raked over his nipples and they sprung to life, hardening, hot and eager.

"It wasn't all that hard to track a heavily bleeding man being dragged along the ground." Christian barely glanced at their primitive surroundings. "The tricky part was finding this chamber and figuring out a way in. I finally occurred to me to watch the monkeys coming and going and then I followed them. It was a snap."

"A snap, huh?" Brandon ran his fingers through Christian's hair, ruffling it and tugging it when they caught in the occasional tangle. Christian didn't seem to mind. Each pull on his hair seemed to make the fire in his eyes glow brighter. "I think your mind's snapped." He laid a line of hard kisses along Christian's jawline, nipping at the soft skin on the underside. "Why did you come after me?" It was a pained whisper that turned into an angry admonishment. "I might have been dead!"

"Shut up." Christian shut off any response by taking Brandon's mouth in a brutal, crushing kiss. "If I hadn't come, you *would* be dead. Besides, dead men don't keep bleeding for hours. I wasn't leaving you behind."

The second kiss was just as raw, but this was long and deep, fists on both sides of the embrace grabbing handfuls of shirt, skin, and hair, both men desperate to reassure themselves the other was alive while clinging onto the solid evidence of that fact.

Passion, rough and uninhibited, ignited with the first touch of their lips. Any lingering reservations either man harbored about Kamat watching them disappeared like morning mist on a hot summer day.

Brandon caught glimpses of Kamat as she silently came to stand by the altar, her body close enough that he could smell her flowery scent and see the lust and longing in her black eyes. As his hands roamed and rubbed roughly over Christian, removing clothing and discovering skin, he felt fleeting light touches from hands he knew belonged to her, but he didn't care. Nothing could stop him. His heart, body, and soul needed to be loved, and Christian was the only one who mattered. She could experience their lovemaking, but she would never be a part of their love.

More of Christian's skin was exposed with each discarded piece of clothing and Brandon hastened to assist the pair of helping hands pulling off his pants, underwear, boots, and socks. He ended up on his back on the altar, Christian pinning him to the cool surface, their bodies entwined, hands still roaming freely, urgently, with their mouths sealed together in a hungry, full body kiss.

Tongues pressing and sliding, they both explored and mapped the recesses created by hard teeth and soft lips. The sensitive lining of Brandon's cheeks and roof of his mouth tingled after each slick caress of Christian's tongue. He was on fire with need, his renewed flesh itched, and his cock, hard and eager, ached. His ass clenched at the thought of Christian buried deep inside of him, dick mimicking the bold, forceful action of the tongue thrusting down his throat.

Arms wound around Christian's neck, Brandon pulled on his lover, encouraging Christian to roll on top of him more fully. When Christian moved between his thighs, Brandon locked his ankles at the small of Christian's back and thrust up, rubbing hard cock to hard cock.

The need to reaffirm love, life, and commitment burned bright in his chest. A wave of something he could only describe as primitive, raw emotion swept through him and he attacked Christian with a voracity even Brandon knew was uncharacteristic for him. He broke the spine-tingling kiss and nuzzled at Christian's neck and jaw, leaving teeth marks in his wake.

A low growl rumbled from the corner where the lion lay and Brandon found himself mimicking the sound, a fierce desire to dominate and claim bursting to life in the pit of his stomach. His hands gripped Christian's hair in a hold that said nothing sweet or gentle and he reclaimed the man's mouth in a bruising kiss again. He felt strong, powerful, and undefeatable.

Christian's hot skin rippled under his palms, muscles working as the man's biceps moved, hard abs heaving with each panted breath or needy groan. Visions of Christian holding off Kamat and her lion to protect him, and then bargaining with the vampire to save his life flashed behind his closed eyelids, mingling with glimpses of their previous lovemaking and stolen moments of laughter and affection.

Brandon knew without question Christian was the partner he had been looking for all his life. A man who wouldn't give him up, who would fight for him in ways Brandon could never have predicted.

If faced with the events of the last twelve hours, Phil would have run out on him long ago, just like Phil had run out on him by choosing Susan. Marrying a woman was easy, safe, and comfortable. Phil was all about cutting his losses and coming out the winner in life. Brandon had never been so happy to not be a part of Phil's world.

Christian gave as good as he got. Taller and stronger than Brandon, he used his physical advantages to take control of the moment, pushing Brandon's shoulders to the slab with his weight. Christian's chest crushed Brandon's torso flatter under him, one hand entwined tightly in Brandon's hair and one under Brandon's ass, gripping, kneading, his fingers working their way into the crease between his cheeks.

And all the while their mouths ravaged each other in a clash of teeth, tongues, and lips that left chins bruised and a corner of Brandon's mouth bloodied. Grunts and heavy pants filled the silence of the chamber, the scent of flowers occasionally mixing with the smell of blood, sweat, and male hormones. Pre-cum faintly added to the warm, humid air and aided the frantic, harsh rut and bang of groin being ground and thrust into groin.

His knees were grabbed on either side by Christian's hot, sweaty hands and forced higher, the act lifting his hips off the altar, raising his ass and spreading his cheeks in one swift, fluid motion. Both their cocks were covered in a thin coat of slick fluid, but entry now would be difficult and painful. Unexpectedly, a small hand wormed between them and something thick and sweet was massaged over both their straining, dueling shafts, the added stimulation sinfully thrilling, the addition of a forbidden act. Christian's well-prepared cock butted against his tight hole and it clenched and relaxed, anxious and rebellious at the same time, wanting to be breached, while his own cock strained, eager to find a hole of its own to plunder.

Primal need crashed over him and Brandon struggled, consumed by a sudden desire to be the invader, the alpha male, the dominant partner, and for a moment the two men were equally matched, kissing, holding, pushing, pulling, yanking, pounding flesh, each seeking the upper hand until they both pulled back far enough to look the other in the eye. Then a silent communication passed between them and Brandon surrendered control, knowing without speaking that Christian needed this to convince himself that Brandon was alive and truly his lover.

Christian raked the flat of his tongue up Brandon's neck and plunged his cock into his lover, sinking in to the base of his shaft in one harsh thrust. Brandon groaned and bucked, forcing Christian deeper, the gut-wrenching, burning pain a delirious sensation that sent streams of pulsing pleasure along every nerve ending and fiber. Not waiting for any sign from Brandon that he had adjusted to the abrupt entry, Christian began thrusting in a rapid, pounding rhythm that jarred delicious bursts of white-hot excitement to Brandon's cock. Reaching down, Brandon fisted himself, mirroring the hammer-like stroking in and out of his asshole.

The slap of flesh hitting flesh was an irregular, frenzied beat. Christian's balls and thighs impacted hard against Brandon's ass, his shaft sliding long and deep into Brandon's spread, clinging hole. The rapid, vicious action made Brandon's teeth chatter. He raised up enough to latch on to one of the dusky, swollen nubs on Christian's chest to stop the clatter.

Mouthing the firm tit, he teased it, first sucking it hard, then rolling it between his teeth, biting it with a strength that made Christian growl at him. The sound made his stomach tighten, his hips thrust faster and his ass flutter and burn around the thick cock battering into him. He did it all over again to the other taut nipple just to hear the growl repeated.

Their grunts and moans, groaned whimpers and low, rumbled growls filled the night and the chamber room. Brandon was faintly aware of light, ghostly touches on his skin and the occasional glimpse of Kamat's entranced face or outstretched hands circling the table, but for the most part he was only conscious of Christian lying above him, stroking inside of his body and filling his mind and heart.

Other voices echoed in his head, a few of which he could only feel but not hear. He sensed these voices had no words to speak, so he tried to mute them, knowing they were the untamed beasts in his blood, their emotions too wild, too violent to be given full rein. The deep rumble he made in his own chest when his climax began to build told him they had a strong voice in his responses anyway. He licked his way over salty skin and bulging muscles to Christian's mouth and plunged his tongue down his lover's throat just as his cock shot off, his fist pumping rigorously to pull every droplet of liquid bliss from his orgasm.

His ass spasmed and his hips shoved upward, impaling himself on Christian's cock, his raw opening grinding in a twisting motion on Christian's inward thrust, forcing the ring of sensitive muscle to widen and grip the thickest part of the battering shaft. This sent a burning sizzle directly to his spurting cock and up his spine.

Christian stiffened and groaned, face frozen in a grimace of pain, his cock buried deep in Brandon, the shaft pulling against Brandon's inner walls, bathing them in a wash of cum, marking him with Christian's scent. After a moment suspended in time, they both collapsed, arms and legs tangled together, heads laid forehead to cheek, heaving chest to heaving chest.

The voices in Brandon's head quieted and exhaustion overtook him. He didn't know how long he lay there, but he awoke in Christian's embrace. Tucked at Christian's side, Brandon lifted his head from his lover's shoulder and smiled up at him. They didn't seem to need words yet, the temporary blood connection still weaving their emotions, if not their thoughts, together. Brandon slid more tightly against his lover and began a slow teasing of cock over cock again, having awakened with an erection that belied his weary state and earlier climax.

With a smile and a wink, Christian drew Brandon back down to his side and resumed studying the altar around them, one hand joining Brandon's in a game of tug and stroke with both their cocks, apparently content to enjoy the foreplay.

Absentmindedly, Christian gripped the edge of the altar and his thumb traced the deeply carved design that bordered the entire altar.

Brandon ran his hand up to meet Christian's, the cool, smooth texture of the polished stone against his palm providing a balance to the heat in their other hands as they stroked each other's cock. The glide of hot, silky skin against and over the iron hardness of their dicks rubbing side by side sent ripples of pleasure and anticipation deep into Brandon's abdomen.

Christian frowned and made a humming sound. "They're words, not just designs. A religious chant or ritual incantation." He sounded distracted, barely aware of what he was muttering. "A curse, maybe."

Brandon could see the portion of Christian's mind that was his scientific part detaching a little, a corner of his consciousness becoming preoccupied with the new discovery. Brandon shifted his position, bent a little awkwardly and sucked Christian's cock down his throat to its base. The gasp from above and the sudden grip of fingers woven tightly in his hair told Brandon he had succeeded in pulling Christian's attention back to where it belonged -- on him.

Hands flowing in a continuous motion, one palm after the other down the silky shaft, Brandon sucked the head of Christian's cock into his mouth and traced the underside with his tongue. He lapped at the smooth, domed tip, jabbing the end of his stiffened tongue into the tiny slit to taste the salty reward of droplets of pre-cum. He finger Christian's sac as he sucked, rolling the two small orbs between his fingers and palm, tugging them down, then sliding his hand behind them to rub and stroke the strip of tender flesh that led to Christian's opening. Without warning, he pushed a fingertip into his lover's ass at the same time he plunged his mouth and throat down over Christian's cock, deep-throating the man. He swallowed rapidly to add blinding pleasure to the stab of sharp pain.

Christian moaned and wove his fingers into Brandon's hair, holding Brandon's head in place while his hips bucked up and down.

Brandon loved the feeling of Christian's cock down his throat, his lips stroking the sides of Christian's shaft, his tongue rubbing the underside of the bulbous head, the spongy tip hammering the roof of his mouth, and the groans of need and lust coming from Christian's mouth. It made him feel desired and powerful.

He worked his finger deeper into Christian's ass, searching for and finding the small nubby gland hidden inside. A few well-timed strokes over the nugget and Christian cried out and stiffened. Bitter ropes of white nectar emptied out on Brandon's eager tongue. When he had sucked Christian completely dry, he crawled up to resume his earlier position in Christian's waiting arms.

Christian kissed him, a long, gentle, lingering kiss that held none of the frantic urgency and wild untamed passion of their lovemaking. It was a lover's kiss that spoke of untold nights of love and a future full of promise. When the kiss ended, they sat up and looked for their captor.

Brandon eyed the flare gun, but stopped himself from making a move for it. His vision was blurred and objects were indistinct, like it had been when he was drinking the blood mix, but Brandon was fairly sure Kamat had swayed to one side of the altar to stand and stare at the two of them. A part of him was terrified by her, but another part was unconcerned.

Christian pulled a few pieces of their discarded clothing toward them, raising his pants in the air toward Kamat. "Okay if we get dressed now? Experience enough to earn our freedom?"

She was silent for a long moment – the silence so long that Brandon was sure she was going to renege on their agreement -- but then she nodded and stepped back from the altar, the dark lion close to her side.

As they dressed, Christian returned Kamat's bright stare, curiosity burning in his eyes. "How did you come to be here? You weren't the first guardian, were you?"

"I have been guardian of the temple of Karttikeya for over nine hundred years." Kamat's voice was wistful and hollow, her gaze distant and dark, full of unshared memories. "So very long." She raked her gaze longingly over Brandon's and Christian's still bare chests. "Nine centuries I have been denied the joy and wonder of a lover's touch or passion."

Glancing at the chamber's stone alcoves and ancient carvings, Christian said, "This temple is older than nine centuries."

"Many centuries more, yes." Kamat's face was hard and pinched as if she had remembered something distasteful.

With a flash of insight and curiosity, Christian wondered out loud, "Who was guardian before you?"

Kamat studied them a moment, hands stroking over the lion's broad shoulders and occasionally into its dark, almost ebony, mane. "You have earned the right to know a little of the history." She paused, with a look of yearning Brandon had not thought her capable of bringing a stab of sympathy to his chest. She looked lonely and sad. "You have shared a part of your lives and love. It is only right that I share as an equal."

The lion stirred, growled low and ominously, but Kamat crooned in his ear and he laid down at her feet, his massive head and shoulders still high enough so she could reach them as she, too, sat down on a square chunk of stone from a long fallen pillar.

"The first guardian was a warrior named Manmadharao. He was a powerful man who knew much magic, both light and dark, for one must know thy enemies well to defeat them. He was a great general in Karttikeya's battles, helping his god's final quest to destroy the sacred enemy."

Kamat smiled mirthlessly, her eyes reflecting an understanding that only came with centuries of life. "As a reward for his dedication and loyalty, Karttikeya granted Manmadharao eternal life and honored him with the duty to protect this temple for all time. Manmadharao accepted the honor, never foreseeing the day when the gods would no longer remember him and the temple would to fall to the ruin you see now." She made a sweeping gesture that encompassed the chamber. "Still, Manmadharao was chained forever to his task, unable to leave, commanded to guard the temple and its hidden treasure, the sacred statue of his god Karttikeya for all time."

"Where is he?" Brandon was taken with the story, seeing the ancient gods and their warriors in his head. Imagining it as it might have been during its prime, the chamber transformed to a state of grandeur and religious ceremony that was striking in details. He suddenly realized the flashes of images in his mind were Kamat's memories. Even now he was still connected to the vampire. He wondered how long the link would last, if he would ever really be rid of her influence once they left this place.

"Why are you now guardian?" Brandon glanced at Christian when the man spoke. He got the distinct impression Christian was experiencing the same mental images as he was by the way the archaeologist was gazing around the dark ruins with a look of awe and curiosity on his face.

Voice suddenly stronger, full of pride and arrogance, Kamat straightened her already rigid spine marginally. "I was churel for untold centuries before this temple was built, brought into the darkness by my lover, made whole and powerful by the one creature who loved me above all others." Passion and power reverberated in her speech and coursed along the threads that tied her emotions to Brandon, making him ache with the intensity of them.

She was staring into the lion's face as she talked, gaze examining the depths of the large, tawny-colored eyes that looked dispassionately back at her. "I alone possessed his heart as he possessed mine. We were as one, united in blood and passion. We ruled the night for so long I cannot remember the years, but gradually, after countless deaths and centuries of change, we yearned for an end to our eternal life. We desired to take back our human existence and let our lives conclude as they were meant to."

"Can that happen?" Brandon looked at Christian for an answer before he realized it was probably not one of the man's areas of expertise. He had become so accustomed to the archaeologist explaining cultures, languages, animals, and ancient ruins to him, he was expecting Christian to know the answer to everything. "Vampires turn back into humans?"

Christian shrugged. "Who knew there really were vampires?"

"As churel, I have learned that the mysteries of the dark world are endless. Anything is possible." Her dark eyes moved from the beast's and targeted Brandon. He felt his skin tingle and a flush rise in his neck. "You have experienced my powers to heal. I am but churel. Ancient and powerful, yes, but still only churel. Would you question the power of a god? Have you not come here to gain the power of the statue of Karttikeya for yourselves?"

"We came to India for the statue, yes." Christian picked up his discarded shirt from the ground and handed it to Brandon, then he slipped his pocketed vest over his own bare torso. He looked to Kamat, then smiled appreciatively at his lover. "But I came to the temple for Brandon."

Kamat nodded. "The statue attracts people in love. That is its power. When my mate and I heard of the statue of Karttikeya hidden here in this sacred temple, and of the powers it was reputed to have over love and life, we knew we had found the answer to our need. Tired of our never-ending existence, our fondest desire was to be returned to human form. We sought the statue of Karttikeya to have it granted." She scanned the chamber, taking in the monkeys, the broken pillars, bloodied altar and lastly, the great, patient lion at her side. Her head drooped low and her voice trembled slightly as she added, "We were not successful."

"There were two of you." Christian's tone was hushed and gentle, as if he was asking about a recently deceased acquaintance. "What happened to your lover, Kamat?"

She straightened, eyes overly glistening, but voice once again full of regal privilege and determined strength. "He remains at my side, and I at his." Hands still buried in the lion's thick mane, Kamat brushed her cheek lovingly against the lion's face and he butted her head gently in response to the caress. Both Brandon and Christian gaped at her.

"Ahmedabad?" Brandon heard his voice and the surprise in it, but something stirred in mind and he remembered the sensation of the beast flashing through his mind, filling his heart and desires with a ferociousness that could have only come from a wild animal. He knew the answer to his next question even before he asked it. "He's your lover?"

"He is my heart." It was a simple statement but it carried the entire sum of Kamat's reason for being. Brandon could hear the weight of her unwavering loyalty and love in her passionate, trembling voice.

Ahmedabad rose and stood between the men and Kamat, his closeness making Brandon uncomfortable. It was difficult not to remember the nightmare of being attacked and mercilessly dragged through the unforgiving jungle, shoulder gripped in the beast's jaws, each jarring step through the underbrush torturous agony.

"What happened to him?" As if he could read Brandon's uneasy thoughts, Christian moved closer and casually slung an arm behind Brandon. Brandon felt the heat from Christian's skin touching his back. It was comforting in the face of the animal that had almost fatally maimed him. Christian continued with, "I assume Ahmedabad was human before?"

"He was." A smile lit her face, then faded. "Though still faithful to his god and his sworn duty to see the statue and temple protected, Manmadharao had also wearied of his lonely existence. When he learned of our quest, the strength of our love for one another, and our true natures as churels, he saw an opportunity to escape the isolated purgatory his own magic had not found a way to resolve. Knowing we would live forever as he now did, and so could guard the temple for all time as Karttikeya had commanded, he placed a spell on Ahmedabad using his own warrior blood--" Once again she stared into the beast's somber, unblinking eyes. "--turning my love into the dark beast you see before you.

"The accursed spell was performed here, on this same altar, as we slept through the sunlight hours." Kamat's small hands gripped the edges of the stone slab until her knuckles were white and a small piece of the altar snapped off under the force of her grasp. She turned back to face her companion, his sable fur rippling as he instantly, instinctively, moved silently to her side once more. "Ahmedabad is forever linked to this temple and the surrounding jungle, his memory of who and what he was before he was locked away, with only his unshakable love for me remaining." Her eyes had glazed over with a faraway look that was now filled with hatred and contempt. "Manmadharao was a cruel man."

Kamat smoothed the fur of Ahmedabad's face back from his eyes and snout with loving strokes, voice wistful and sad. "We can not share our love as we once did, as we are meant to share it. As he is, he cannot take my blood at the peak of our joining, the way all churel achieve the ultimate joining. Our love has remained locked away inside. Together for eternity, yet always apart. Inseparable, but irrevocably separated."

Brandon felt her immeasurable sorrow and longing like a tangible ache that stole his breath and squeezed his throat. He remembered what it was like when he thought he would no longer be able to have Christian in his life. Intolerable to the point of agony. He knew Christian felt it as well by his pained expression. Neither spoke. Kamat continued. "Ahmedabad has been cursed. He can never take human form. Never take his churel shape. And I can never leave him."

She buried her face in his black mane, but no sound escaped as her shoulders shook, hands fisted in the tufts of ebony fur. Brandon was at a loss for words of comfort that would mend centuries of loneliness.

"'Dark Beast'? 'Blood of warrior'?" Christian snapped his fingers and moved to stare at the altar inscriptions that had distracted him earlier during their lovemaking. "Wait a minute. I read something about that." He ran his hands across the stone edges, fingers tracing the deep cuts of the undecipherable ancient text.

Although Kamat remained seated with her head on Ahmedabad's, she turned her face to watch Christian.

Brandon could see Christian's mind working, knew the archaeologist had discovered something important to them by the excitement in his voice and his eager, preoccupied look.

"It's a spell. I'm sure of it. I've seen writing similar to this before, studied it a little even, but honestly, I shouldn't be able to read it. But I can. A part of me now understands this. Something has given me the ability to grasp an ancient language so old, there is no record or sample of it left in existence outside of this temple chamber." He glanced from Kamat to Ahmedabad, then upward to the chattering troop of monkeys. "My money is on the lutung's blood."

He used his palm to wash small pools of Brandon's blood from the middle of the altar out to the sides so that it ran into the carved letters. Once the dark liquid filled the cuts, the symbols became clearer and Christian began to read out loud. "'With the blood of a warrior, by the will of the gods, let the dark beast emerge...'"

Leaning over to watch Christian examine the ancient scribbling, Brandon's fingers slipped into one of the carved symbols on the altar. It was full of blood, his blood, from earlier. The blood was still warm and fluid. He rapidly yanked his hand back when he thought he could feel something -- the stone altar or maybe his blood -- pulse against his fingertips.

"Whoa!" He hurriedly wiped it on the leg of his pants, leaving a dark stain on the khaki fabric.

"What?" Christian's head shot up at the sudden action, worry and mild impatience evident.

"For a second there I thought it ..." Brandon paused. He couldn't tear his gaze from the table. "It pulsed." He raised his blood-tinged hand, holding it out for Christian to see.

"What pulsed?"

"M-my blood. The old stuff that leaked into the carved symbols."

At this, Kamat stood and rushed to the altar. "Manmadharao's blood pulsed when it flowed across these symbols where he cursed Ahmedabad." She drew her fingertips through the still flowing liquid, excited, eyes wide and glistening. "I feel nothing."

Brandon and Christian both tentatively slipped a finger into the cold blood, but nothing happened. Brandon murmured, "Read it again. It happened when you were saying the spell, or curse, or whatever the hell it is."

Christian repeated the altar phrase and both he and Brandon jumped and removed their hands when a definite pulsing sensation rippled in the blood.

Only Kamat seemed delighted by the new development. "The dark lion was given form from Manmadharao's warrior blood and Ahmedabad's body. No matter how many centuries I have studied these symbols, I have never been able to understand their meaning."

"I believe I can break the curse."

"Do not offer false witness, Chris-*ti*-an. I am not a forgiving woman."

"I can break the curse. The text is an ancient spell. At least half of it is. But the other half is the counter spell, a reversal chant. All I need is Ahmedabad and blood. We have both of those."

"It will not work with just any blood. It would have to be a warrior's, and we have no warriors here."

"That's where you're wrong. You have your fingers playing in a warrior's blood right now." He indicated the altar where Kamat was lazily rubbing her hands over the blood-filled engravings. "Brandon is a police officer, a 'modern warrior', so to speak. You can feel his blood pulse with the power of the spell. It knows he's worthy, that his blood has the power to activate the spell."

"You can do this?" Excitement and an anxious anticipation lit Kamat's beautiful face, but underneath Brandon could tell she was afraid to truly believe. Ahmedabad had approached and stood at her side, great tongue lolling out to lick at a few droplets of red that had trickled over the edge. One of her bloodstained hands fell to caress the flat strip of his wide sable forehead. "You can give me back my heart?"

"We can try. Brandon's blood has already been spilled on the altar." He palmed more of the shimmering blood into the cuts in the stone surface. Kamat swiftly joined him and after a moment's hesitation, Brandon assisted, careful not to let his fingers linger in the tiny puddles he was creating.

"I can read the spell; that, along with your churel powers, will make it work." Christian's excitement grew, but he glanced around at the monkeys overhead and down to the ring of symbols in the stone. "But we need to do it soon before the effects of the blood I drank dissipate. I think I only know how to read the symbols because of the knowledge in the animal's blood. Once that's out of my system, I'm pretty sure the knowledge will be gone, too."

The efforts of all three of them had made short work of filling the symbols and now all of the ancient, until now indecipherable, signs stood out in dark relief against the cool, gray altar.

Both Brandon and Christian rinsed their hands off in the basin of water that remained on the ground from earlier, while Kamat licked the blood from one hand and allowed Ahmedabad to lick the other clean for her. Catching sight of their actions, Brandon quickly busied himself with cleaning out his nails.

Wiping his wet hands on his pant legs, Christian motioned to the altar where he and Brandon had made love to earn their freedom from this dark pair. "Can you get Ahmedabad to stand on it?"

She nodded, softly spoke a few words Brandon couldn't understand in the lion's ear, and the massive beast launched his over six hundred pounds of muscle, fur, teeth, and claws onto the three-foot high stone slab. He stood in the center of the altar and growled at Brandon, teeth bared and dark eyes staring, nostrils flaring at the renewed taste and smell of the detective's blood.

Brandon held his ground, something undefined and confident telling him the lion would not attack again. It was unnerving to see into the animal's primal desires, but far more disturbing to actually understand them.

Despite both the churels' previous deadly behavior, Brandon couldn't hold it against them. He understood what desperation and fear of being alone or losing a lover was like. He knew what it could do to a person's reasoning. He'd already demonstrated the outlandish lengths he was willing to go to for love by being here. So had Christian when he'd tracked Brandon and his attacker through a dangerous jungle alone and broken into a sealed temple chamber. Brandon didn't regret accepting the Collector's request to obtain the statue of Karttikeya from this lost and lonely temple, but it hadn't turned out the way he had envisioned it.

Christian held out his hand to Kamat and the vampire joined him at the end of the altar. They stood facing Ahmedabad. Kamat made a downward gesture with her open palm and the lion dropped to the stone, regally lying down, the altar dwarfed by his bulky frame.

Brandon stepped back a pace and quietly picked up the discarded flare gun. If this worked, he wasn't sure what to expect from a vampire newly released from the body of an animal where he had been imprisoned for almost a millennium. His cop instincts screamed "be prepared" while a newer part of his brain whispered from a dark corner "don't be afraid." He decided to have the gun handy and the shadowy thoughts gave a sigh. He was beginning to hope the effects of the shared blood would wear off soon. Very few detectives who listened to voices in their heads kept their jobs.

With a "take no prisoners" glance at both his companions, Christian waited for a nod from Kamat, then slowly began to recite the altar text out loud, pausing every few words so Kamat could repeat them. Her arms were stretched out toward Ahmedabad, her wide-eyed stare piercing her lover, eyes once more solid orbs of black. Her skin turned a lighter shade of bronze that shimmered and glowed brighter with each word she called out into the cool chamber air.

For once, the monkeys were silent; no movement or sound drifted down from the vines and ledges above them. Brandon glanced up. Their pinched little faces seemed frozen in expressions of anticipation and fear.

The chamber room was suddenly cooler, the walls appeared closer, the shadows between the flickering torches grew longer and unnaturally deeper. The air turned thick and heavy, making it slightly difficult for Brandon to breathe. He knew Christian was experiencing the changes too, when his words faltered slightly during the chanting. Even Ahmedabad drowsily lowered his head to rest it on his forelegs and closed his eyes, possibly asleep. Kamat alone seemed unaffected.

The chanted words, both Christian's deep tones and Kamat's lighter, singsong echoes, seemed to rush through the air in gathering swirls, growing larger with each new phrase, spinning wildly around the now senseless lion. The words rose up from the blood-filled symbols, dark droplets in a twirling whirlwind that flashed and glowed a ghostly hue of dazzling red. They pulsed and shimmered around and around Ahmedabad until they had completely encircled the massive beast, obliterating him from view.

Kamat's voice grew louder, her tone more urgent, repeating the chant again and again, her power building, the strain visible in the pained grimace etched into her fine features. Christian had finished and he stepped back from the altar, gaze darting between Kamat and the altar. Brandon tried to look into the whirling top of magic and blood, but could see nothing else.

Kamat cried out, repeating the chant one last time and then collapsed. Christian caught her and held up while she regained her feet. Looking exhausted but expectant, Kamat slowly pushed out of Christian's arms and looked toward the altar.

The whirlwind spun faster and the blood trapped in it pulsed louder, the audible rhythm increasing to a thunderous beat that grew until Brandon made to cover his ears. Then suddenly the glowing mass exploded into a flash of blinding white and was gone.

Faster than Brandon could adjust his eyesight, Kamat darted past him. He heard a faint swishing sound and a gentle thump. When he had blinked away the last of the blinding effects of the explosion, he saw Kamat effortlessly pull a tall, muscular, naked man to the edge and help him tumble to the ground and into her waiting arms. She immediately settled to the floor of the chamber and crushed the unconscious man to her. He saw pink tears filled her eyes before she buried her face in the man's long, thick hair.

As Ahmedabad tumbled off the altar, the center of the stone slab came alive with an eerie glow. The ring of text trembled, then with a grating sound of stone grinding against stone, the ring rose on three pillars of rock to reveal a platform on which a small golden statue rested. Kamat gasped and Brandon and Christian gaped at the sudden, unexpected discovery now revealed to them.

None approached the altar or tried to touch the statue, but Kamat regained her powers of speech first, voiced hushed and reverent.

"The sacred statue of Karttikeya. It has been unattainable during all our years of guarding its hiding place. It was revealed only once, when Manmadharao cursed Ahmedabad. It granted his fondest wish – to be released from his sacred duties. I have struggled unsuccessfully to call it forth for nine centuries. I can not believe it is within my grasp now."

"Take it, Kamat."

Her disbelieving gaze raked over both men. "Do you not wish to possess the statue and its power? Have you given up on obtaining *your* heart's desires?" She stared at Brandon first, then Christian.

Shaking his head, Brandon beamed at Christian as he answered Kamat. "I've already got my heart's desire, thanks. Don't need the statue anymore."

Christian returned the warm, brilliant smile for a long moment, then gave Kamat a less intimate grin. His face and tone reflected a quiet gratitude. "You gave me mine when you saved Brandon's life." He slipped an arm over Brandon's shoulders.

Brandon relaxed a little into Christian's side, his gaze wandering to Kamat's newly transformed lover. He studied the still unconscious Ahmedabad wrapped tightly in Kamat's embrace. His dark head was pressed against her breasts, her cheek flush to his forehead, her dark eyes still brimming with pink tears of elation. "I think being separated from your one true love for over nine hundred years entitles you to the statue. You and Ahmedabad have earned it."

Mouth parted in wonder, she closed her eyes and rocked back and forth, clinging to his body. One small hand brushed the dark hair back from his deep bronze-colored skin to rub at his temple, a curious expression of concentration and joy on her face.

Brandon had the strangest feeling that although Ahmedabad was unconscious, the two of them were communicating. It struck him that he was watching an act more intimate then having Kamat watch Christian and him make love. He averted his gaze to look up at Christian.

"What about finding your father, Chris?"

Christian frowned a little, but his voice was determined and confident. "We'll just have to look the old-fashioned way." He pulled Brandon closer. "I know this good-looking detective who tracks down and sorts out clues for a living." Brandon gave a wry smile that broadened when Christian firmly added, "After this, I think we can do just about anything if we stick together."

"You sure?"

"I'm sure. If you're up for helping me."

"I'm good with that." Brandon wrapped his arms around Christian's waist and fitted his hip and thigh against the other man's groin, rubbing back and forth with a teasing pressure. "Just how close do you think we should stick together?"

"I think this close might do the trick."

"I was hoping we'd agree on that." Brandon moved his hands down to rest on Christian's ass.

"Compromise. That's what a relationship is all about."

"Hmm." Brandon smirked. "Interesting, but I was thinking a compromising *position* was needed here."

Christian snorted a laugh. "At least one." Christian dipped his head down to capture Brandon's lips in a kiss, but Kamat's voice captured both of their attentions.

"You may have the statue."

"Say again?" Brandon couldn't believe his ears. She was giving up her chance at the dream she had nurtured and suffered so much to gain for nine centuries just like that?

Kamat pointed at the statue. All three faces of the Hindu god shone in the light, its gold surface polished and smooth, the multiple raised arms tangled like dancing snakes, the peacock so detailed Brandon could almost imagine its rich jewel-toned feathers and regal crown bobbing with each step it might take. It looked exactly the same as the one that Phelan had shown him at the Collector's home. But this one's power radiated off it in ripples that he imagined he could see if he stared at it long enough.

"The statue is yours. We no longer have need of it. We have much time to make up for and mortality has lost its attraction. We choose not to experience mortal death but to explore our regained life. Suddenly eternity together does not sound so tiresome."

"You're sure? Ahmedabad is sure?"

"We are in agreement." Ahmedabad's lips twitched and Kamat gently kissed them before continuing. "When you take possession of Karttikeya, there will no longer be anything here to guard. Duty to the gods has been satisfied. A warrior has returned and rightfully claimed the statue with his blood offering. It is yours."

She clapped her hands; the unexpected sharpness echoed off the stone chamber walls as a section of impenetrable wall dissolved into a huge archway connected to a long hallway Brandon guessed led to the outside world.

Kamat smiled, clutched Ahmedabad to her chest, and added, "Use it wisely."

Christian beat Brandon out of the door by a half a pace, their hands clasped tightly together.

CHAPTER THIRTEEN

"You did exceptionally well, Detective King." Dr. Andrew Martin, the famed and mysterious "Collector," nodded once at Brandon. Then his pleased glance lit on Christian. "And Dr. Carter." He tilted his head graciously toward the archaeologist, gaze taking in every aspect of Christian's appearance approvingly. "Together you've accomplished a task many others have not been able to achieve."

The Collector gazed hard and long at the small gold statue in his gnarled, thin hands. He rotated it slowly, a slight tremor evident, though his grip on the replica of the Hindu god was firm, with awed appreciation written on his face and reverence in his wavering voice. "You've done well. Very well."

The imposing mansion looked exactly as it had the first time Brandon had seen it. The lawns were perfectly manicured, the brass door accents still gleamed, and the same formal butler answered the door when he and Christian had arrived. Nothing had changed, but everything was different.

The only addition to the grand setting was the Collector himself. Spine ramrod straight in the wheelchair, the Collector held his head high, an Old World elegance emanating from his gracious demeanor and precise, cultured voice. The man's pale coloring was slightly ashen, but a bright spot of pink bloomed in his cheeks when Brandon presented the coveted statue to him. His eyes sparkled with life, in direct contrast to his obviously weakened, aged body. He was more than a little surprised to notice that although the older archaeologist's gaze was primarily fixated on the gold figurine, it frequently, though less blatantly, wandered to study Christian.

Knowing the archaeologist was as eager for an introduction to the legendary Collector as the older man was to receive the final addition to his totem collection, Brandon was pleased Christian had been permitted to accompany him to the meeting.

It had been a long and exhausting journey made more pleasurable by the luxurious, and secretive, transportation home that the Collector had arranged for them.

Once they had escaped Kamat and the temple and made it back to their village hotel on the outskirts of Madhya Pradesh, there was no time for them to recuperate from the grueling trip back out of the jungle. They had found a jeep with an impatient driver waiting for them, courtesy of their benefactor. From there they ended up in an unmarked helicopter that whisked them off to a private airstrip. They were spirited from one private jet to another until, ultimately, worn and weary with jet lag, they arrived on home soil and were delivered to their meeting with the mysterious Collector at the Wisteria Hills estate. No customs officials ever saw them or the small, coveted statue from the lost temple of Karttikeya, but their passports had been stamped and signed by a silent, black-suited man who accompanied them on all of the flights.

Brandon desperately wanted time alone with Christian, but he was ecstatic to be back to civilization. He made their driver stop at a convenience store for a large bag of his favorite candies and then insisted they turn around to use the drive-through window of the first coffee shop they passed. A handful of Sparkles and a king-sized cup of coffee made it tolerable for him to face the possibility of recounting the harrowing story of the statue's discovery. He hoped no one would care once the Collector was presented with the figure, and Brandon wasn't disappointed. The archaeologist's interest seemed limited to Karttikeya and Christian.

"It was..." Brandon traded a wry look with Christian. "...an interesting trip, but I'll spare you the tedious details." He shrugged, giving the Collector a small, sardonic smile. "You probably wouldn't believe them anyway. Now that we're back home, I'm not sure *I* believe all of it." He glanced at Christian again, but this time it was with an affectionate smile on his lips. "But it was worth it--" His gaze darted to the Collector's beaming face. "--even if I almost died."

There was a sharp, feminine gasp. Audra Phelan stood protectively at the aging Collector's side, one hand possessively on his thin shoulder. She seemed pleased that Brandon and Christian had returned, but an almost palpable air of apprehension clung to her as well. She, too, seemed to steal covert glances at the younger archaeologist; her prim expression now appeared to be tinged with curiosity.

Brandon had to admit, even rumpled and weary, Christian was a very attractive man. His jeans hugged his hips and nice ass just right, showing off his muscular thighs and long legs, and his faded, blue denim work shirt, open at the neck with partially rolled up sleeves gave him a rugged, casually confident look. The waves of dark hair framed his face and brushed against his tanned neck and strong, shadowed jaw, and softened the weathered lines at the corners of his clear gray eyes. Brandon wasn't surprised other people took notice of the handsome man when meeting him for the first time.

"Are you sure you're all right, Detective?" Ms. Phelan scrutinized Brandon's face and body, looking for signs of injury. Brandon suddenly wished he'd worn something nicer than a polo shirt and jeans, both of which were hanging a bit looser on his slight frame than they had before his trip to the lost Hindu temple. He was sure his plain appearance lacked Christian's charismatic flair or the Collector's cultured air.

"It was close, but I'm fine." Suddenly self-conscious, Brandon shrugged. Aware the concern was genuine, but unwilling to discuss vampires and transformed lovers, he kept his explanation purposefully vague. "I fell into a trap. Christian found me. He saved my life." He shot his lover an intimate, playful look. "In a lot of different ways." He pulled his stare away from Christian and addressed the Collector. "I wouldn't have made it back here or gotten that statue if it hadn't been for him."

Ignoring the undisguised scrutiny from the other pair, Christian stepped closer to Brandon to rub an open palm over the shoulder that Ahmedabad had viciously maimed and Kamat had mystically healed. Brandon noticed Christian did that a lot since their return. He found it comforting, almost a reassurance he was healed and whole again. He assumed the gesture did the same thing for the other man. It was a touching show of unspoken affection that didn't go unnoticed by anyone.

The Collector reached up and squeezed Phelan's hand where it still rested on his shoulder, his eyes watching as Brandon automatically leaned in closer to Christian.

"The right men for a dangerous, difficult job. A modern warrior was needed. Brandon, your survival skills as a police officer and your professional ability for assessing evidence fit the bill perfectly." His expression clouded over briefly. "Much better than any of the military men did in the same situation."

With a tilt of his head, the old archaeologist's steady, intense gaze locked on Christian's face. Brandon thought the Collector looked a lot like Christian did when he got that inscrutable, piercing glint in his eye. He guessed it was an archaeologist thing, examining people and objects like they were bugs under a glass. "And a scholar with the knowledge of ancient civilizations and the guts and field experience to put them to use."

Christian beamed at the compliment, the bright smile lighting up his face and washing away a little of the tired wrinkles around his eyes. "It's long been a dream of mine to meet you, sir. I'm a big fan of your achievements. I can only hope to have as accomplished a career as yours." He looked at Phelan, then back at the old man. "I'm honored to have been a part of the excursion, but I'm curious as to why I was chosen for it."

He frowned a little as Phelan and the Collector exchanged cryptic glances, but neither answered. "You are the one who sent the information to me, right?"

Until now, both Brandon and Christian had remained standing in the great room. While they waited for the others to join them, they had spent time admiring the artifacts and paintings on display. Brandon had been content to keep moving and occupied to prevent him from falling asleep in one of the high-backed, deeply cushioned chairs or the overstuffed couch. No one had insisted they sit, and Brandon was hoping for a short visit to turn over the statue, let Christian meet the Collector, then immediately head home with his lover. Unfortunately, now that the introductions were complete and the statue handed over, the Collector seemed to have more on his mind.

"I had Audra extend the offer to you, yes. I knew you'd be unable to resist the challenge, Christian. Brandon needed your expertise if he was to accomplish his quest." He gestured to the couch and both men hesitated before politely taking a seat.

The older man's expression became a mix of sadness and regret. Brandon thought he suddenly looked older than he had when they arrived, almost as if he had just remembered a horrific, long ago event. There were tears in the man's eyes.

"And I confess, Dr. Carter--" Dr. Martin's now watery gaze never wavered from Christian, his voice strong but betrayed by a small tremor from time to time. "*I* wanted you to go."

Dr. Martin stared at Christian's silent, confused face for several moments before gently adding, "I thought I owed you the chance to be truly happy. Have a family of your own." His gaze flickered to Christian's right hand where it lay on the cushions, subtly resting on top of Brandon's left hand. There was no condemnation or disgust on Dr. Martin's face. "I wanted to give you the opportunity to achieve your heart's desire, whatever or whoever that might be." A small smile tugged one corner of his mouth up. The pleasure Brandon heard in his voice was reflected in his brightly shining eyes.

"Why would you care? I've wanted to meet you for years, to try and learn something about my own father's whereabouts, but--" Christian gave Brandon a wide-eyed shrug. "--I've never met you before today. Why would you owe *me* anything, sir? Forgive me, but I'm confused."

"I owe you a chance at happiness because... I'm the reason your mother died, Christian." The Collector looked at Phelan, caught her sharp nod, then continued before a stunned Christian had a chance to comment. "I'm the reason you grew up with your aunt and uncle. I care..." He took a deep breath, then let it out slowly. "...because I'm your father, young man."

"My father is Dr. Andrew Martin, *the Collector*?" Christian slumped back into the cushions. A flash of anger set his full lips into a straight line. His gray eyes were cold and hard as he stared into his father's sad, dull eyes. Dr. Martin sat stone still in his wheelchair, breathing coming a little harder, his color now pale and ashen, one hand tremulous, his thin shoulders beginning to stoop. Christian's anger dissolved as they stared into each other's faces. It was replaced with a growing astonishment and wonder. "I can't believe this."

Brandon stood up, confused and unsure of exactly what was happening. He frowned at the wheelchair-bound man. "You never told me any of this. What are you playing at, Doctor?" He felt deceived by the old man and his prim, silent assistant.

"Carter is my mother's maiden name. I've always used it."

"Yes. After her untimely death, my wife's sister didn't want my son to have any connection to me, not even my name."

"*You're* my father." Christian released Brandon's hand.

"Not too disappointed, I hope."

Standing beside Brandon, Christian shook his head. "Not disappointed at all. I've... I've followed your career when I couldn't find any more evidence of my father. I didn't even suspect you and he were the same man." Christian glanced around the opulent room, his gaze discarding the luxurious furniture and priceless paintings to linger longingly over the archaeological artifacts and finds displayed in cabinets and cases. "My only regret is I'm sorry I missed out on being a part of your life all these years. Part of your experiences and amazing discoveries."

"It wasn't by choice, Christian." Dr. Martin's voice wavered and cracked as he said his son's name. "I knew your aunt thought your mother's death might have been prevented if I'd come home to be with her when you were born."

He sighed, his gnarled hands turning the statue of Karttikeya over and over again. "I understood she didn't want you to see me. I respected that. She was a good woman who gave you a wonderful, stable home full of love and affection." He was fervent and sincere in his conviction he had done the right thing. "Something *I* could never give to you."

The statue became still in his lap, one arthritic thumb rubbing absentmindedly over the little gold god's multiple smiling faces. "Then time passed--" He gestured helplessly at Christian's tall, broad frame. "--and you were suddenly a grown man, establishing an enviable career and gaining an impressive reputation for acquiring artifacts all your own. Following my footsteps!" He looked up at a silent Christian; a glow of pleasure and pride lit his face, his voice a strained, emotional whisper. "I am so very proud of you, Christian, so *very* proud."

Seemingly at a loss for words, Christian knelt and hugged his father, fierce and long, his expression as painfully sad and regretful as Martin's had been earlier. Christian released his hold, adding a squeeze to the old man's thin shoulders as he pulled back, a half-hearted smile on his lips and tears of his own blurring his gray eyes.

Brandon was glad he didn't need to speak just now because he doubted he could.

Martin's wet gaze moved to meet Brandon's where it lingered for a moment before the old man smiled and looked back at his kneeling son. "And I'm pleased you found someone who makes you happy, Christian. My entire motivation for getting you to go with Brandon was to have the statue of Karttikeya help you to find your heart's desire. I wanted to be *sure* you were happy before my life was over. I just didn't know I'd sent you the man who'd do that for you!"

"When I started out on this quest, my heart's desire wasn't to find happiness for myself. Maybe the statue did have something to do with bringing us together, but I think Brandon's and my feelings for each other happened without the statue's influence."

Christian watched his father's expression cloud over. He clasped one of his frail wrists as Martin's hands still clung to the heavy golden god. "My fondest desire was to find *you*. Before there wasn't any time left to get to know one another. I knew your health was failing." He paused a moment. When he continued, his voice choked on the last few words. "I just didn't realize how little time we had left."

"Even less time you think, Christian." Martin's voice was weaker and his breathing was becoming shallow and labored. He seemed to shrink before Brandon's eyes.

"What? Why?"

"You've brought me the means to right the wrong I did thirty-five years ago when I left your mother to give birth to you on her own. I didn't realize how frail her mental state had become over my long absences. I was preoccupied with wondrous discoveries and puzzling ancient mysteries. So much so that I forgot the living needed my attention as well." He handed the statue to Phelan. "With this last piece, you and Brandon have amazingly provided for me, I can finally make amends to your dear mother."

"You want to bring her back from the dead?" Alarmed, Christian laid a hand on the statue.

"No, nothing so unattainable." He patted Christian's hand, then gripped it with his own and pulled Christian's hand to his chest, to his heart. "*My* heart's fondest desire is to have my wife's forgiveness." Martin glanced up and found a waiting Phelan a few feet away. "Audra?" He gave her a beseeching look and an affectionate smile.

"I'm here, Drew." She came to him and gently, briefly, caressed his sunken cheek with one strong, long-fingered hand, and then guided his wheelchair over in front of the center of display case. She remained with him at his side.

Her actions forced Christian to move. He stood on the other side of his father, one arm motioning for Brandon to join him, which the detective hesitantly did.

Martin looked up at Christian. "I'm so sorry to have missed being a part of your life, but please know you were always in my thoughts and heart. I've been a part of you, from a distance, all your life. This--" He pointed a bent and bony finger at the surrounding room, encompassing the rich splendor and the ancient discoveries. "--has all been for you." Not waiting for a response, Martin handed the gold statue to Phelan.

All three men watched in anticipation as she placed the figurine onto a large pedestal in front of the display cabinet. She opened the thick glass doors and slowly backed away, gaze riveted to the collection of eclectic objects within. By the time she had retaken her place at Martin's side, the statue seemed to emit a dazzling light all on its own.

Taking her hand, Martin drew Audra Phelan down until he could place a fond kiss on her lips, then he softly said, "You have been my dearest friend and my closest companion. I leave my work and my son in your capable hands. I know you love them both as I much as I do. You know my wishes."

Wordlessly, Phelan nodded, then kissed Martin's forehead and patted his cheeks with both hands before resuming her place at his side, one hand on his shoulder, to watch the events she had just set in motion continue to unfold.

One by one the previously retrieved artifacts, all fabled to be a part of the mystical love totem, began to glow until it was difficult to see the individual objects at all. Brandon blinked several times and shielded his eyes from the brilliant lights, but he was sure each artifact was somehow shifting and changing, melting like an ice cube on a hot summer sidewalk, changing form, their now liquid masses running together and merging. With a sudden flare of blinding white, the streams of liquid suddenly coalesced, re-formed, and hardened, all without a single touch from human hands.

The flare died away and on the pedestal where the liquid had reformed stood a phallic shape, four feet tall. It looked like a milky white crystal with rounded edges. It stood on its own, perfectly balanced on the flat pedestal, though its bottom was completely spherical.

Hand trembling, Martin reached out and touched it before anyone could stop him. The crystal vibrated and a low hum penetrated the room. The hum sent a ripple of excitement through Brandon's entire body. Christian grabbed his hand and held on tightly, seemingly determined not to take any chances on being separated again.

A small dot of light appeared in the center of the crystal, then grew and expanded until it was like a beam of light from a powerful flashlight, the stream of white luminescence filling the space between Martin and the crystal totem. Out of the shimmering glow stepped a young woman, slender and delicate, with Christian's dark wavy hair and beautiful marbled gray eyes. She was pale, almost translucent. No one in the room could mistake her for a living being. Her skin glowed a soft milky white like the crystal. She seemed to be unable to talk, but her gentle gaze and expressive face spoke volumes. She radiated love and understanding. Even Brandon could feel it.

She gave Christian a wide delighted smile, but she only had eyes for Martin. Wordlessly she reached out a hand to him and he grasped it.

"Penelope, my love. I have waited so long to see you again." Martin's voice broke and the tears trickled down his gaunt cheeks unheeded. "So long to tell you how much I love you." He brought her hand to his lips and kissed it reverently. "I have been privileged to know other joys and other loves, but though all the thirty-five years you've been gone from my life, you have remained my true heart's desire."

Brandon looked up at Christian to see how his lover was handling this extraordinary event. The man had a wide, sad smile on his face and tears on his cheeks. It had to be hell to find both of your parents for the first time in decades, only moments before losing them forever. Brandon sniffed and leaned closer to Christian. A heavy arm slid across his shoulder as Christian pulled him tightly to his side.

Penelope backed away a step, bringing Martin out of his chair with her. His steps were unsteady and slow, but he seemed to gain strength with each one. When her back was to the opening of light, she stopped and cupped his face with her free hand, a soothing caress that spoke of forgiveness and shared memories. Her fingers trailed over his mouth, tracing the line of his upper lip again and again in a lover's touch.

Eyes closed, Martin sighed and clasped her hand to his face, taking in a ragged breath through her fingers, seemingly lost in her scent and touch for one intimate moment. Then he opened his eyes, his breathing more labored and a grimace of pain on his face, one hand clutching his chest. She lowered her hand from his face, his fingers clasped in hers, and began to back into the light from where she had emerged. Each step Martin took drew him further and further into the glow and he began to change, his spine straighter, his hair darker, and his parchment skin becoming a healthy tan.

Just before he stepped through the opening, Brandon could see Andrew Martin as he must have looked as a young man -- tall, proud, and charmingly handsome. Christian had inherited his mother's eyes and dark hair, but he was his father's son in every other physical aspect. And then the man was gone.

The instant Martin's disappeared, the totem blazed, consumed by a silvery flash of energy and light. The air crackled and the hum became deafening as the crystal began to crack. A dozen shards of white hung suspended in the air, then one by one they disappeared into thin air, each winking out of existence. The light faded and empty air was left in the totem's place on the pedestal.

"What happened?" Both stunned men turned to Phelan for an explanation.

"Andrew got his fondest wish." Phelan's voice was shaky, but she stood tall with her head high and a wistful look on her tearstained face. "He was granted Penelope's forgiveness and a chance to be with her at last."

"And the totem?" Christian wanted to know.

"A love totem's purpose is to unite lovers, to grant a heart's fondest desire. It can only do that if it is out there to be found. Each time it is made whole and its most powerful, final wish is granted, it breaks apart and scatters itself through time, space, and the universe to be retrieved again."

"I'd say I don't believe it, but after meeting Kamat and Ahmedabad, I'm open to a whole lot more than I used to be."

Brandon wrapped an arm around Christian's waist possessively, grateful he'd been given his second chance with Christian while they were both still alive.

"What will you do now, Ms. Phelan? Will you keep in touch?" Christian touched the woman's shoulder, and Brandon could see the concern and caring in his face. This woman was Christian's only link to his father's life and memory. Brandon could understand why he would want to keep it open.

"Call me Audra, please, both of you. I've been writing to you since you were old enough to read, Christian." She smiled at the both of them for the first time and Brandon felt a burst of warmth for her. She was remarkably attractive when she smiled. "I think we can be on a first name basis now."

"Audra, then." Christian graciously conceded. "I know you made his dream your work. What now?"

"Now--" She looked at the empty pedestal and drew in a deep breath. "--I continue the quest. The foundation that funds this project is separate from your father's personal holdings and, with your permission, I'll continue his dream. I'll help twelve new people who are desperate to find their heart's desire."

Nodding, Christian asked, "And when you have all twelve again?"

Audra Phelan gave a mysterious smile. "I may just have my own fondest desire to ask for."

◊ ◊ ◊ ◊ ◊

The coffee mug was oversized, thick-walled and heavy, great for holding in heat. It wasn't a traditional mug. This had the look of an ancient ritual chalice, which Christian suspected it was. It was certainly hundreds of years old, maybe more. He had been against Brandon using it to gulp his daily ration of blistering coffee, but eventually relented, giving in to Brandon's assertion it had been gifted to them to be used, not stared at. A set of two mugs had arrived shortly after they had moved in together. It bore a postage mark from a small province in southern India. There hadn't been a card, but the two men knew who it was from.

The sides were engraved and decorated with a pattern of symbols and letters that depicted the four elements of the earth and another that nobody would recognize who hadn't been touched by the dark world of ancient legends and mystic souls. It was a pattern that was burnt into Christian's and Brandon's memories. No matter what it had stood for before, it was now a symbol of their commitment and love for each other.

Even though it was their usual routine on the weekends to laze around in bed and enjoy each other, Christian had slipped out early without explanation, leaving Brandon to sleep in. The weather had turned cold and dreary, and Brandon had curled up to enjoy the warmth Christian had left behind. When the sheets turned cold, he had gotten up to start his day.

The apartment door opened and closed, but Brandon didn't move away from the coffeemaker. He always drank the first cup in front of the machine, then refilled his cup again to sit down and read the morning paper. He wasn't going to ask where Christian had been. It didn't pay to be too nosy this time of year.

He glanced at the kitchen doorway, enjoying the sight of his sexy partner as he sauntered in, handsome face still deeply tanned despite the winter weather, his strong cheekbones highlighted by a rosy tinge and windblown curls that strayed onto his forehead and neck.

"You're up. I got you a present." A sudden chilled kiss landed on the back of his neck, making Brandon shiver, both from the cold and the thrill of kiss.

"What for?" Even after all this time, simple gestures of affection from his lover still surprised and excited him.

"Christmas isn't for two more weeks." Brandon reluctantly put down his coffee to pop the last of the sugarcoated candies in his hand into his mouth. Wiping his palm off on his jeans, he accepted the white envelope Christian offered with a dramatic flourish.

"Just open it and find out." Christian grabbed the abandoned cup and stole a sip of the robust, dark brew. Brandon grabbed it back and put it down out of Christian's reach.

Puzzled, Brandon ripped the large envelope open and withdrew a sheet of fine linen paper. He stared at it, then at his lover, confusion still written on his face. "One hundred shares of Newt Industries stock?"

Christian picked up one of several discarded wrappers from the top of the wastebasket by the end of the counter and flashed it at Brandon. "They make Sparkle Candies. I'm surprised at you, Detective. Addicts usually know their suppliers, babe."

Surprised and delighted by the unexpected gift, Brandon laughed and looked closer at the certificate. "Awesome! Weird gift, but awesome." Voice intimate and warm, he gave his lover of the last four months a deeply pleased grin. "You're insane. Thank you."

Christian grabbed Brandon's wrists, plucked the papers from his hands and tossed them onto the kitchen counter. Spinning Brandon around, Christian pulled him into his arms and backed him up to the wall. "I think they'll make a great yearly gift."

"Nice, but I don't think I'd want the same thing *every* Christmas."

"They're not for Christmas." He pecked a quick, hard kiss onto Brandon's lips.

"No?" Brandon kissed back, just as hard, but a lot slower.

Christian pulled his lips away only far enough so that his words could be heard. "Nope. I thought it would make a nice wedding anniversary gift each year."

Brandon paused for a moment before he breathed a soft "You did?" into Christian's mouth.

"I did." Christian grinned and wiggled his hips, making Brandon hiss and squirm against him in frustration, still pinned to the wall. "I thought we could have the flower girls toss coffee beans down the aisle at the church instead of rose petals, and wedding guests could pelt us with handfuls of Sparkles after the ceremony." His grin widened. "All environmentally friendly."

Laughing, Brandon grabbed his lover by the ears and shook his head. "You really are insane."

Undaunted, Christian asked, "So, what do you think?"

After staring into his lover's marbled gray eyes for several heartbeats, reading the love and sincerity in the intense gaze, a smile lit up Brandon's face.

"Coffee, candies, and Christian, the three things I can't live without. I think…" Brandon pulled Christian's head down so their lips brushed. "…I think, *I do*."

ABOUT THE AUTHOR

LAURA BAUMBACH is an award-winning author of erotic romance and fiction. Named best M/M writer of 2006, she captured 3 Top Ten Preditors & Editors spots in 3 different categories for 2006 and her scifi adventure romance is nominated for an EPPIE award for best GLBT novel of 2006. Her favorite genre to work in is manlove or gay erotic romances. Manlove is not traditional gay fiction, but erotic romances written specifically for the romantic-minded reader, male or female. Author of numerous novels, screenplays, and short stories including Alyson Books' Ultimate Gay Erotica 2007, Laura has also written erotic stories for several magazines.

Laura's won the coveted EPPIE Award for best GLBT novel of 2008 for *The Lost Temple of Karttikeya*.

Visit Laura on the web at:

www.laurabaumbach.com